Sharing Charlotte

Club Zodiac
Book Seven

BECCA JAMESON

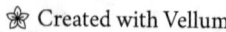

ACKNOWLEDGMENTS

Totally have to thank my amazing assistant for everything she does for me and for kicking me in the butt to get this one written. She is the best! Love you, Michelle.

CHAPTER 1

Charlotte nearly jumped out of her skin when she heard a throat clear behind her. She spun around quickly, hand on her chest, heart racing. "Shit," she muttered.

Samson stood leaning against the frame of the door to the master bedroom. He looked far too casual, one hand holding a bottle of water at his side, the other stroking his chin. His slightly longer brown hair was pulled back in a band at the nape of his neck. He was wearing a black tank top with his gym logo on it and black mesh shorts. Black gym shoes rounded out his outfit. He wore this exact uniform nearly every day of the week.

What made her heart stutter was the one raised eyebrow.

She swallowed and lowered her gaze. "Sorry, Sir. I didn't realize anyone was home."

"I see that." He shoved off the frame and sauntered closer. "There are two problems with this picture. If you can list them both quickly, I'll consider keeping my palm from straying too low on your thighs when I spank your bottom in about thirty seconds. I know it embarrasses you when your

1

skirt isn't low enough to conceal my pink palm prints from your coworkers."

She swallowed, a shiver making her entire body twitch. "I'm sorry, Sir. You're right."

What the hell had she been thinking? She knew the rules. She rarely broke them. She'd been on a mission when she rushed home in the middle of the day, and not expecting anyone to be home, she'd made an error in judgment.

It would be futile to give excuses though. That wasn't her style. No excuse was good enough. She licked her lips, kept her gaze to the floor, and spoke in a clear voice. "I should have removed my clothes the moment I entered the penthouse and left them at the front door."

"At least I know you don't have amnesia," he joked, though his voice was anything but teasing. "And?"

"I should not still be fully dressed now." She reached for the buttons on her white blouse and rushed to push each of them through their holes. As soon as she shrugged out of the silk material, she unzipped her navy pencil skirt and let it fall to the floor. By the time she kicked off her heels, slid her thong down her legs, and unhooked her bra, she was a ball of nerves.

Master Samson hadn't spanked her in several weeks. She'd obviously broken her streak today.

Charlotte didn't mind being spanked when it was an intentional part of a scene that would end with her getting off, but when Samson spanked her for punishment, he didn't mess around. He would leave her pale skin burning and pink, his palm prints obvious to anyone who saw her ass.

The only someone who would be seeing her naked butt in the near future would be her other Master, Nile. He would undoubtedly get a call from Samson this afternoon and come home well informed.

Samson lowered himself onto the bench seat at the foot of

the king-sized bed and reached out a hand. "Come. Let's get this over with first, and then you can explain to me why my submissive is home in the middle of the day breaking rules."

She took a breath as she shuffled forward, bracing herself for the stinging burn that was about to land on her ass.

When she got close, Samson wrapped his hand gently around her elbow, positioned her at his side, and urged her to drape herself over his lap.

She knew the drill. It wasn't difficult. She bent at the waist and situated herself over his warm thighs, her breasts hanging between them. She even gripped her hands at her back before he ordered that next step.

"Good girl." His hand rubbed her butt.

She was always amazed by his ability to remain so completely calm and gentle when he punished her. Trying not to stiffen, she drew in a breath and exhaled slowly. The problem was that there was very little difference between Samson's two types of spankings—the one for pleasure and the one for punishment. Sure, he might strike her a bit harder and faster when he was disciplining her, but the result would be the same. She would end up aroused.

Being naked and draped over his thighs already had her pussy wet and her nipples tight. The way he warmed her ass up before he started was driving her arousal higher by the second. As soon as he swatted her, she would gasp, her pussy pulsing with need.

Charlotte braced herself as Samson removed his palm from her skin. Sure enough, a moment later, he swatted her bottom hard enough to make her gasp. She'd been spanked plenty of times, but it never ceased to shock her system.

He continued, shifting his hand around as he spanked her to ensure he left no skin untouched. She didn't bother to count, but when he finally stopped to rub her burning ass, she figured he'd given her about a dozen quick swats.

Samson held her steady over his thighs for several moments, rubbing the sting until she finally resumed normal breathing. Finally, he helped her to stand and pulled her around in front of him. "There. Done." He tucked her hair behind her ear and nudged her chin up so that she met his gaze.

"Wow. What did I miss?" The new voice belonged to Nile, and it came from behind her, making Charlotte blow out a breath.

Great. How the hell did both her Masters happen to be home in the middle of the day?

Samson turned toward Nile. "We haven't gotten to the *why* yet, but for some reason our little sub arrived a few minutes ago and beelined for the bedroom without a single care in the world for the house rules."

"Ah," Nile said. "That would explain why her clothes are lying on the floor in here instead of neatly folded by the front door. Guess she didn't expect anyone to be home." Nile chuckled as he set his hand on Charlotte's shoulder and then ran it down her back to cup her heated ass cheeks.

"I'm sorry, Sirs. I wasn't thinking." She leaned slightly into his touch.

"Or..." Samson responded, "you didn't think you needed to obey rule number one because you thought you could just sneak into the house, accomplish whatever mission you were hell-bent on accomplishing, and race back out without anyone being the wiser."

"Yes, Sir," she whispered. He was right. She hadn't wanted to take the time to remove all her clothing at the front door, rush into the master bedroom to grab a weekend bag, and then put all her clothes back on. Apparently, she'd errored.

Nile took a seat on the lounge next to Samson, leaving her standing naked in front of them. They both had an amazing ability to assert their authority even while looking up at her.

She shuddered as her body betrayed her, coming alive sexually while she was being reprimanded. The way they looked at her, dominating her from the bench they sat on, made her clench her pussy.

"Now," Samson said. "Mind telling us what you rushed home to do?"

She wanted to ask them the same question. Granted, one or both of them sometimes came home for lunch, but neither of them had mentioned doing so today specifically. She needed to face the fact that she hadn't been thinking. She'd been so distracted that she hadn't even noticed Samson was already in the penthouse when she entered.

She shifted her gaze back and forth between them. "I need to go to Denver for a few days, Sir. I thought I'd rush home and grab my stuff." Charlotte owned a chain of three upscale boutiques in Seattle. She was looking to expand to Denver, her hometown.

"Did you find a possible property?" Nile asked.

"Yes, Sir. My realtor found a place that just became available. She's afraid someone might grab it fast, so I need to go take a look."

"That's good news. I'm surprised someone put a property on the market this close to the holidays." Samson set a hand on her hip and then slid it to her lower back.

Frankly, she was shocked too. She had assumed it would be January before she heard from the realtor. As for needing to leave town for business, neither man would be angry. They all three had careers that took priority in their lives whenever necessary. It was partly why they were such a good match for each other. They were busy. Even on weekends. With Charlotte owning three stores, Samson a gym, and Nile a catering business, weekends were just like any other day to them. Since there were three of them, usually no one was left completely alone for long.

5

They had an arrangement. It worked. When they were outside of the house, they were professionals. When they stepped through the front door, Charlotte left her high-stressed boss mode at the door and submitted to Samson and Nile. Always. No matter who else was home. Even if she was alone, she submitted to them inside the house.

Except today.

"When's your flight?" Nile asked.

"Eight, Sir. I was going to text you in a few minutes."

"Are we making you late for anything important?" Samson asked.

She shook her head. "No, Sir. I was just rushing like I always do. No particular reason." The truth was that lately all three of them had been so busy that Charlotte hadn't experienced much dominance from either man. She wasn't sure if they'd grown complacent or if their arrangement was waning. That latter idea was depressing, but something had felt off for a while now. She couldn't put her finger on it.

She wished they would both pull her into their embrace right now and fuck her senseless. It would ease some of her stress. But that wouldn't happen, not after being disciplined.

"How many days do you think you'll be gone?" Nile reached around her, threading his fingers with Samson's at her back, tugging her closer in the process. At least they both had their hands on her. They still cared. She knew they did. Any doubts she had were unfounded.

"Not sure, Sir. If the place doesn't suit me at all, I'll come back tomorrow. If I decide to make an offer, I'll probably stay the weekend."

"Okay. Let us know. I can probably rearrange my schedule for the weekend and join you if you decide to stay. I catered an event here in Seattle once for one of the managers of Club Zodiac, Colin Wynne. We could go check it out. He said to contact him if I was ever in town."

"I've heard of Club Zodiac, Sir. It's relatively new, isn't it?"

"Yes. It wouldn't have been there when you were growing up."

She giggled. "I wouldn't have known one way or the other at the time, Sir." She hadn't joined the fetish community until she was in her mid-twenties, about five years ago. After a lifetime of quietly believing there was something seriously wrong with her, she had gone to Seattle's premier club, Surrender, with a girlfriend. Her friend had only gone out of curiosity as a lark, but Charlotte had immediately known she was home.

"True." Nile squeezed her hand. "Either way. I'll call Colin and let him know you'll be in town. If I can't get there by Friday, go check it out."

"Yes, Sir." She shivered inwardly. Was Nile being polite in sending her alone? Or was he losing interest and trying to get her to find someone else? The truth was that Charlotte loved the fetish scene. Passionately. She'd known from that first moment she entered Surrender years ago that she was submissive and immediately joined the club and started frequenting it every time she was available. There was no doubt she liked to play more than most people. Preferably daily. That was the reason she'd ended up living with not one but two Doms.

A lot had changed in her life in the past five years since that day she found herself, but her love for the club scene was still alive and flourishing. Her current arrangement suited her fantastically, but she was concerned about whether or not it still suited both of her Doms.

When she met Samson's gaze, he had that brow lifted again. His serious authoritative side always made her horny, though she'd never tell him that out loud. Unnecessary instructions were coming next. "Don't go running off thinking what happens in Denver stays in Denver."

"Yes, Sir." She flushed. They had an agreement. She would never break it.

Samson continued. "Nile will make sure his friend knows what our rules are. Panties on. Keep your hands to yourself. No one touches your pussy."

"Yes, Sir." She squirmed. They trusted each other. There were times when one of them went to Surrender without the others. They all enjoyed playing. But when they'd entered into this living arrangement, they'd included several boundaries. No man was permitted to touch Charlotte's pussy without specific instructions and supervision from either Nile or Samson. In addition, neither of them were permitted to touch another woman in that way.

The reverse was also true. Samson and Nile kept their packages covered, while Charlotte kept her hands off other men's junk.

Charlotte had a huge sexual appetite. She liked to get fucked often. Having a steady relationship with two men ensured her needs were met. Keeping the boundaries they'd set ensured no one got exposed to STIs and added a level of commitment to their arrangement.

It worked for all three of them.

Nile wrapped an arm around Charlotte's waist and hauled her between his legs. His palms were warm, spread across her back, and she moaned softly when he suckled a nipple. She let her eyes drift closed as his tongue swirled around the tip, teasing her. She knew he wouldn't let her orgasm—not so soon after being spanked—but it felt delicious to have his mouth and hands on her.

Samson joined Nile, leaning from the side to take her other nipple between *his* lips. He reached between her legs to nudge them wider apart as he tormented her, but he didn't touch her anywhere she craved.

The frustration mixed with arousal would keep her on edge for hours. They knew it. She knew it. She also loved it.

Finally, first Samson and then Nile released her nipple with a pop. Nile spoke. "Guess we better get you packed. You're going to need warm clothes. It can be colder in Denver than Seattle in December. I think it's supposed to snow this week. Maybe we can sneak in some Christmas shopping on Saturday." He smiled at her, eyes wide. When it came to Christmas, Nile was like a kid. He enjoyed decorating and surprising people with gifts. Samson wasn't as interested, but he indulged both of them.

Nile stood as he cupped her chin and then leaned down to kiss her lips. "It's too bad you broke the house rules. I bet you're going to leave here squirming."

She shifted her weight from side to side. He was right. If only she'd taken the time to remove her clothes and put on her robe when she entered the house, she'd probably have both men inside her right now instead of a burning sting on her ass coupled with a burning need between her legs. Because she'd made that poor choice, she was going to be horny for the next several hours.

"Call us when you get to your hotel tonight," Samson added. "FaceTime." He lifted that brow again.

She released a breath, knowing he would make that call worth her while. Both of them were excellent at phone sex, and they enjoyed watching. Maybe they would let her get off tonight. Maybe they wouldn't.

Samson nodded toward the closet. "Go get packed."

"Add the pink vibrator," Nile suggested. He pushed to standing. "Never mind. I'll help pack."

Not surprising. Nile was the most organized one of the three of them. He often had a hand in her clothing choices.

Charlotte smiled as soon as they couldn't see her face. The

pink vibrator was by far her favorite, especially when she was alone.

CHAPTER 2

"Hi. You must be Charlotte." The man smiling at her was not what she expected. He was younger and sexier. Nile hadn't mentioned how old Master Colin was, but for some reason she'd pictured someone in his fifties.

She took his hand. "Yes, Sir. Master Nile told me to ask for you."

He gave a firm shake and then motioned for her to follow him through the door on the other side of the entryway. "Come on in. I'll show you around. At Nile's request, I've arranged a scene for you."

Charlotte smiled. Of course he did. Nile thought of everything. Nile also liked to control things. Sure, he wrapped it up in a nice package making it seem as though he'd done her a favor, but she had no doubt he'd left Master Colin strict instructions about the sort of scene he would permit Charlotte to participate in.

If she were a different woman, she might be aggravated, but instead her nipples stiffened under the lacy black push-up bra she wore. Samson was by far more of the disciplinarian in their arrangement, while Nile was the organizer. Both made her shiver.

She loved the control they had over her. She loved that Nile planned what she did and when and where and with whom. He'd even packed the outfit she had on right now while she'd chosen the clothes she'd needed to meet with the realtor.

And Samson? She loved that she couldn't get away with anything. He had eyes in the back of his head. If she didn't obey the house rules, he knew it. Every time. Ensuring she didn't disobey her Masters was sometimes challenging, but she found she enjoyed the rewards a day with a clean slate provided as well as the discipline from a day with a few points against her.

Punishment and then denial was Samson's specialty, and denial meant she came even harder when she was finally permitted to reach climax. Both were winning scenarios.

Unfortunately, neither man had mentioned the pink vibrator nor given her permission to come last night when she called. They'd discussed a number of things ranging from the schedule change their house cleaner needed to a leaky faucet in the guest bathroom. Charlotte had ended the call feeling slightly let down and empty. She'd curled into a ball on her side under the covers, but sleep hadn't come immediately. Instead, her mind had gone on a tangent, worry consuming her about the status of her relationship with both men.

It wasn't something specific she could put her finger on. She didn't even want to bring it up with them because she felt ridiculous even worrying. But she'd felt a slight distancing lately. Even though she reminded herself they'd all been preoccupied with work—which was always busier for all three of them during the holidays—it felt like more than that.

By all reasonable rights, she should point out her concern and call for a group meeting. They'd agreed when they made this arrangement almost three years ago that they would all be open and air out anything on their minds. Easier said than done.

Forgetting where she was, Charlotte nearly ran into the back of Colin when he stopped just inside the main room of Zodiac. She lifted her gaze to take in the expansive area. She knew this club was relatively new and that the owners had another club in Miami. That being said, she was impressed with the size and the décor. It was painted black—not surprising—with lighting angled toward each apparatus that could be adjusted to suit the desire of the Dom or Domme. All the latest equipment was available. High end. Clean. Professional. Not unlike the club she belonged to in Seattle —Surrender.

Colin led her around the room, pointing out some of the recent additions with pride before he led her to a bar area on one side of the room. He helped her onto a stool. The edge of the counter was adorned with tiny, colorful, twinkling Christmas lights that added a festive mood to the corner of the room. The reception area had vomited Christmas. Every inch had been covered with lights and decorations and even a small tree. But this main room gave no indication of the holiday except for the strand of lights around the bar. "Would you like something to drink? We don't serve alcohol, nor do we permit outside alcohol, but just about anything else."

"Seltzer please, Sir." She perched on the seat, back straight, ankles crossed, hands in her lap—exactly as her Masters would request if they were here.

Seconds later, the bartender handed her a tall glass filled with the sparkling ice water.

"Nile suggested you might enjoy a flogging scene, so I made arrangements with one of our best floggers. I think you'll be pleased."

"Yes, Sir." She forced herself not to fidget on the stool. Nile knew her well. She looked forward to the release she would get from a flogging after a long day, even though it wouldn't include the added bonus of an orgasm. At least when she knew that before starting, she could adjust her mindset.

"I'm sorry Nile couldn't join you tonight."

"Yes, Sir. He had an event he couldn't get out of, but he's flying in tomorrow morning."

Colin smiled. "Great. Maybe you two can join us tomorrow?"

"That would be lovely. Thank you, Sir."

Colin tapped the table with his palm and righted himself. "Well, I need to go find my submissive. Rayne is around here somewhere. You'll be okay for a few minutes?"

"Of course, Sir."

He nodded and left her alone.

Charlotte was glad to have a few minutes to look around and watch. Even though she was far from new to BDSM, every club had its own vibe, and she didn't mind taking the time to get a feel for the type of people who frequented Club Zodiac.

Ten minutes later, someone spoke behind her. "Charlotte?"

She twisted her head around, surprised to find a familiar face as the man continued to approach.

His eyes widened. "It *is* you. When Master Colin told me I would find a woman named Charlotte at the bar, I didn't think anything of it, but when I saw your unique hair from behind…" He'd reached her side, and he cocked his head to the left and narrowed his gaze. "Wow. I can't believe it's you. I haven't seen you since high school. Do you even remember me?"

She swallowed her shock. What were the chances she would encounter someone she'd known over a decade ago in a fetish club in Denver? Of course, her strawberry-blond hair was always a dead giveaway. No one forgot it.

"Yes. Of course. Rex Kyle, right?" She flinched. It was completely inappropriate for her to address anyone by their real name in a club, not without express permission at least. Of course, it was also unacceptable for anyone to acknowledge knowing someone from the real world too, which Rex had done the second he saw her. At least they were even.

He closed the distance between them and leaned an elbow against the bar, waving away what she assumed was complete horror from her expression. "Don't worry. Everyone here knows my name. I don't use a pseudonym. I guess you don't either."

"No." She lowered her gaze. "No, Sir," she murmured.

It would seem Rex was a Dom. She struggled to wrap her mind around that thought. Rex Kyle? A Dom?

"I've changed a bit." He chuckled, speaking as if he'd read her mind. "Or perhaps grown into my true self. Then again, apparently so have you." He reached under her chin and lifted her face several inches. "I'd prefer you look me in the eye while we negotiate."

She met his gaze, struggling to breathe. Rex had been a total brainiac in high school. Obviously that wouldn't have changed. Even though he'd been a bit of a nerd, for Rex it hadn't made him unpopular. He was so damn smart everyone looked up to him and counted on him to help them with whatever subjects they struggled in.

He may have been a dork, but he was friendly and gracious and kind. And...confident. She knew this for a fact because she too had called him for help with physics her senior year. He'd patiently helped her study for her final exam for several hours on two occasions. Thank God, because she'd passed that class, and wasn't at all sure it would have happened without him.

"Why don't you tell me a bit about yourself to break the

ice. Whatever you're comfortable with of course. If it's too awkward between us, I'll find Master Colin and have him rearrange the schedule so you can sub for someone else. Deal?"

"Yes, Sir." She shivered. Calling someone *Sir* in a club setting came second nature to her, but she'd never in her life encountered someone she knew.

"Master Colin says you're visiting from out of town?"

"Yes, Sir. Seattle. I went to college there and never left."

He nodded. "Ah. I've heard nice things about Seattle. Haven't visited myself yet. I went to MIT, but after I graduated, I came back to Denver. I've enjoyed being closer to family."

She nodded, uncertain what he expected her to say next. It was easier to let him ask the questions. She didn't have secrets. Okay, that wasn't true. She did live with two men. She wasn't really excited about telling Rex Kyle that five minutes after reacquainting. Hopefully he wouldn't delve that deep.

"What do you do...Sir? I mean, if you don't mind me asking." She was dying to know what the smartest kid in school who went to MIT did for a living.

He wiggled his brows. "I'm an information security manager."

She drew back a few inches, squinting, her lips turned up slightly in a smile. "Of course you are. Why am I not surprised? What does that mean exactly?"

"Basically, I'm a computer hacker."

"Soooo, you break into banks and move all their money to your account?" she joked.

He laughed. "I could. If I wanted to." He was not modest. "But no. I'm an ethical hacker. Some call us white hat hackers. I work for an agency that places me wherever I'm needed. My job is to break into their systems, find the weaknesses, and fix them."

"Oh. Wow. Never thought about that." She winced, realizing she hadn't addressed him as Sir twice in a row. He didn't comment though.

"I get the benefit of working from home often, but I also travel a lot. It's a growing business. Every big company in the world needs legitimate hackers."

"Yeah, I guess so...Sir. And, you belong to Club Zodiac." She glanced around. It was more of an observation. She was struggling to picture Rex with a flogger. She couldn't reconcile this particular Rex with the guy she'd known in high school.

"Yep. I also belong to another club in town called Roses and Thorns, but Zodiac is larger. I come here often." He cocked his head to one side. "You're having a hard time visualizing me as a Dom."

"Yes, Sir," she murmured honestly.

He chuckled again. "If it's not too awkward for you, follow me and I'll knock every preconceived notion you've ever had about me right out of your mind." He stood taller, lifting both brows.

For the first moment since he'd approached, she saw him as a Dom. She had nothing to lose, so she decided to consent to his proposal. It took a very firm Dom to really top her. She doubted Rex was up to the task. But it would be rude to Master Colin to ask for someone else. "Yes, Sir." She slid off the stool, clasped her hands behind her back, and lowered her face.

As she followed Rex across the room, she let her gaze wander up his torso. He was more filled out than high school. Still slender, but he didn't spend every moment behind a desk. He was taller too. Six feet at least. His hair was the same dark black, but it was cut stylishly shorter than she remembered. His skin was pale, but not more so than hers.

Rex stopped next to a spanking bench and turned to grip

17

her chin with two fingers. His demeanor had altered to one of authority, making her skin tingle. Maybe he *was* up to this task.

CHAPTER 3

Rex stared into Charlotte's eyes for several moments, assessing where she was mentally. He still couldn't believe she was here, in Club Zodiac, about to submit to him.

There was no doubt she was submissive. It came naturally to her. He wondered when she'd figured that out and if she'd had any long-term relationships with Doms or merely dabbled. Considering the fact that Master Colin had personally arranged this scene for her, Rex had to assume she wasn't a novice. Colin would have told him that. Instead, Colin had only requested a flogging scene for a visiting sub. The parameters had been that he leave her panties on, not bring her to orgasm, and not break her skin. That last one went without saying. Rex didn't ever injure a sub or draw blood.

Rex's curiosity was piqued now. After all, he knew Charlotte in high school. She was one of the popular crowd. On the dance team. Pretty. Sought after by all the guys.

He'd known her since junior high and always thought of her as snobby. For six years. Right up until the end of their senior year when she'd asked him for help with physics. He'd nearly swallowed his tongue when she met his gaze after class one day, her soft voice stammering, as if it were difficult for her to ask for help.

That was when he'd realized she wasn't like other popular girls. She was surprisingly kind, friendly, and sweet. She didn't treat him like the nerdy kid he was. She wasn't condescending, nor did she exhibit any indication he wasn't her equal. In fact, she'd fully insinuated he was better than her. He'd been shocked and denied her implication, but it had touched him that she thought he was someone special because he was so smart.

They spent several hours in a coffee shop. It was then he learned that she was also studious and hard-working. She had good grades and had been admitted to several excellent universities. Physics simply hadn't been her strong subject.

Charlotte wasn't just a pretty face. She was also a wonderful human. And she was going to put him to the test right now because damn, she was fucking sexy in a black bustier that gave her amazing cleavage. Her creamy skin made his dick hard as soon as he'd approached. She also wore a black skirt, lacy and full. He had to presume she had something on underneath since he'd been instructed not to remove her panties.

Nope, curious didn't begin to explain how Rex was feeling. Who made these requests? Was she a personal friend of Colin? If so, why didn't Colin dominate her himself? That made no sense. Colin wasn't even around. He'd left Charlotte at the bar and gone in search of Rayne. Perhaps Colin didn't know Charlotte at all and was acting on the request of someone else. Who the hell would that be? Charlotte herself? Possible...

Rex was one of the best floggers at Club Zodiac. He knew it. Everyone knew it. He topped several submissives nearly every night he was in attendance. He always adhered to whatever boundaries the submissive preferred. Clothes on. Clothes off. Partial nudity. Some people wanted the release of a hard flogging up and down their bodies. Some wanted the play to end in orgasm. Rex made it happen.

As he approached the bench he frequently used for a flogging, he turned toward Charlotte to verify her desires. Since he had no idea where the instructions came from, he needed to hear her words. His top priority was always the submissive under his care. At this point, he didn't frankly give a fuck what someone else instructed. His job was to make sure Charlotte was making her own choices. "Master Colin said you were interested in a flogging scene, right?"

"Yes, Sir." She kept her head bowed and her arms clasped behind her back. Her spine was straight, feet spread apart, gaze downcast. She was not new to submission. If he'd had any doubt, it fled the room now.

He lifted her chin with two fingers again. It was important to him that he ensure she was making her own decisions, and the best way to be certain was to see her eyes. "How much experience do you have with flogging?"

"A lot, Sir." She held his gaze.

"How hard do you like to be struck?"

"I can take it pretty hard, but not hard enough to break the skin, Sir."

"I would never draw blood from anyone's skin even if they asked me to. It's not my style."

She nodded subtly even though he still held her chin. Her gorgeous green eyes held his gaze.

"Do you ordinarily get release from the flogging itself, or do you like to orgasm?" He worded that question very precisely.

Her lips parted and then she licked them, hesitating. "I, uh, I don't want to reach orgasm tonight, Sir." He detected a slight shiver.

Interesting. Her response was carefully worded.

He gave a brief nod, deciding he wasn't going to remove any of her clothing either. One of his few instructions had been to leave her panties on, but under the mysterious circumstances, he thought it best to leave her clothed.

It was entirely possible that Charlotte wasn't comfortable being completely naked with a new Dom, nor did she like to orgasm in the hands of a stranger. Or perhaps, she didn't prefer to come in public. However, Rex had the distinct impression there was more to this story.

"Safeword?"

"Red is fine, Sir."

Her submission was flawless. Practiced. She had experience. A lot of it. Maybe she'd been in a long-term relationship along the way. Perhaps she'd just broken something off.

"You're familiar with this type of bench, I assume?" He nodded toward the leather padded bench he intended to use.

"Yes, Sir."

"Please climb onto it, elbows and knees on the pads." He circled her as she did as he instructed, noting she was indeed knowledgeable of this apparatus.

She quickly got comfortable with the center of the bench beneath her, her head turned to one side, her cheek resting on the padding. She took several deep breaths, calming herself.

He paused, watching her face. "Would you like me to restrain your wrists and ankles?"

"If it pleases you, Sir."

Good answer. He opted to secure her ankles, but left her arms free, not wanting her to feel completely restrained for their first scene together, but also not knowing for sure how steady she was capable of remaining. If she squirmed too much while he flogged her, he might not hit his intended spot.

Rex set his palm on the back of her thigh, watching her

reaction as she relaxed into the bench, noticeably not flinching from his touch. Her eyes fluttered as they closed. He considered asking her to hold his gaze for a while but then decided against it. It was possible she felt at least marginally ill at ease having someone she knew dominate her. If that was the case, she might prefer to visualize someone else entirely.

The truth was Rex knew from years of experience that many women liked to go into their minds where their fantasies were hidden when they submitted. It was expected. He rarely denied a woman that pleasure. When it came to sex, he had far different standards. When he slept with a woman, he preferred she be entirely with him, eyes on his, lips parted, every sound intended for him alone.

But this was a scene. Nothing more. A requested flogging from a submissive he just happened to know from his past. If it didn't bother her that they had a tiny blip of history, he wouldn't let it bother him either.

Unfortunately, Charlotte was smoking hot. She'd been the heartthrob of many a guy in high school, and she had definitely improved with age. It was hard to be sure with the bustier she wore, but he felt confident her chest was larger than it had been ten years ago. The rest of her was fuller too. She had an hour-glass shape that appealed to him immensely. And as he smoothed his hand higher up her thigh to expose her bottom, he had to grit his teeth to avoid reacting outwardly.

Charlotte's creamy skin was so smooth and soft, he reminded himself he would have to be gentle with his flogger. Some women had skin that could withstand fairly hard swats. Charlotte wasn't one of them.

Rex flipped her skirt up and settled it on her lower back, exposing her pale cheeks which were mostly visible since the black lace panties she wore covered very little. He'd been instructed to leave them on, but he couldn't stop himself from visualizing what lay beneath. Her puckered hole would undoubtedly be light pink, as would her pussy lips.

This was Charlotte Reilly, a girl he'd developed a crush on when he'd tutored her in high school, and she was currently submitting to him in Zodiac.

Rex mentally shook himself and turned to grab his softest flogger set from his toy bag. Black, supple leather that he nearly always used the first time he flogged someone new to him. If they preferred something more intense, he could switch them out, but he doubted tonight would be one of those nights.

"I'll start light and warm you up gradually," he informed her as he planted himself behind her, letting the strands of leather dangle against the smooth skin of her bottom as he spoke.

She sighed, letting a long breath out slowly. Eager. Ready. Not nervous. She'd done this plenty of times. No part of her was tense, and he was glad she wasn't concerned to have someone unknown to her dominating the scene. She at least seemed to trust him enough to know he wouldn't harm her.

Rex lifted his arms and gently swatted her left cheek with his flogger, switching to strike the opposite cheek in the same manner. He watched her closely, as he did with every submissive, stuffing to the back of his mind the fact that he'd ever known this woman or had any interest in her besides someone who'd requested a scene. It was a mental place he'd learned to go every time he did a scene. Sometimes he dominated women he was sleeping with; other times he dominated strangers. No matter who was submitting to him, they deserved the same level of concentration and care.

Settling into a rhythm where his arms swung comfortably in a figure eight motion, Rex watched Charlotte's skin gradually warm to a soft pink as he landed each soft blow to her pale cheeks and the backs of her thighs. He noted she was at ease, no part of her tensing under his care. Perfect.

After several minutes, he paused and rounded to her side to take her pulse. "You okay, Charlotte?"

"Yes, Sir. Thank you."

"Would you like me to increase the pressure?"

"Yes, Sir." She licked her lips, blinking at him.

He set a hand on the back of her head and stroked it down her soft hair, carefully tucking a loose strand away from her face. Her glorious curls were thick enough and long enough that any Dom would have to secure all that hair high on her head if he or she were to flog her upper back.

Rex glanced at the strands as they fell through his fingers, his mind wandering to thoughts of fisting it and holding her head back, forcing her to look at him. He did nothing of the sort of course, and he removed his hand as soon as he conjured the image.

As he rounded back to her rear, he noticed a few people had gathered to watch. Colin was one of them. He had his hands on Rayne's shoulders. Both of them were watching. Aaron was there too with Hope at his side, one arm wrapped around his. It wasn't unusual for people to watch Rex work, but he didn't usually attract both the managers.

Shaking his surroundings out of his mind once again, he resumed his scene, increasing the force of his strikes as he continued to darken the skin up and down Charlotte's thighs and bottom. She didn't squirm or flinch, absorbing each swat with perfect submission for long minutes.

Finally, she shifted her cheek against the leather bench. He glanced up to see her biting her bottom lip. When he struck her again, easing the pressure, she clenched her butt cheeks and twisted her face toward him. "Yellow, Sir," she breathed out.

Rex immediately came to her side, slightly confused. He

crouched near her face, his hand going to her neck. "Charlotte?"

She swallowed, squeezing her eyes closed for a moment before meeting his gaze. "Too close..." she whispered. "Need a second."

He frowned. Too close to what? Orgasm? He rubbed her neck, concerned about her, hoping to ease the tension at the base of her skull. "Charlotte..." he finally continued, "you're going to have to give me more information."

She took a deep breath, blew it out, and met his gaze again. "I let myself fall under your spell. You're an amazing flogger. I didn't realize I was so close to orgasm."

Ah, so that *was* it. He had to wonder what was so wrong with reaching nirvana if that's what she craved, but he wasn't going to ask. If she wanted him to know more about her, she would tell him.

Rex continued to rub her neck, loving the feeling of her hair against his knuckles, the vanilla scent of it reaching his nose.

Her breathing slowly evened out, and her fingers released their grip on the padded rests beneath them. "Sorry. That's not like me. I can usually compartmentalize better." She offered him a smile.

"No apology necessary. You're entitled to make a scene be exactly what you want it to be and to stick to your plan. I'm impressed by your strength."

He was. She must have had a very compelling reason not to want to orgasm if she had been that close to coming and been able to stop herself and call for a pause.

She let her eyes slide closed again, taking deep breaths.

"I think you're in a nice subspace, Charlotte. Let's call it a night. You need water and time to recuperate."

"Yes, Sir." She sounded a bit chagrined, as if she didn't really want this to end, but between Colin's instructions,

Charlotte's verbal preferences, and the state of mind Rex could see she was in, continuing would only be tempting the gods. If she didn't want to orgasm, and her body was that close, it was time to stop.

Rex tucked his floggers back into his toy bag and then released Charlotte's ankles from the bench. He took her hand and helped her rise onto shaky legs.

She leaned into his side as he led her away from the bench and into an adjoining room that was kept quiet with dim lighting and lots of loveseats. He lowered them onto a leather couch and wrapped a soft blanket around her shoulders. "Hang tight a second. Let me grab you a water." Fifteen seconds after leaving her side, he was back with a cool bottle in his hands, twisting off the cap.

Nothing could have prepared him for the way she downed about half the bottle and then sighed, curling into his side, snuggling against him, even sliding down to set her cheek on his thigh.

As he wrapped his arm around her shoulders and gave her a squeeze, he realized for the first moment since he'd set eyes on her that he was in over his head. He should have known. After all, she had been a fantasy in his mind for years, popping into his subconscious now and then when he least expected it. He'd never dreamed she might be submissive or that he'd ever encounter her in a club. And here she was. In Zodiac, draped over his lap, sated from a flogging he'd delivered.

And she had secrets. Mysterious ones. Secrets he'd love to hear but had no right to pressure her to reveal.

CHAPTER 4

Charlotte had no business snuggling up to Rex like this. She was fully recovered now. She'd definitely gotten sucked into an unexpected subspace from his amazing flogging, but it hadn't taken her long to pull herself back together and shake off the overwhelming need to orgasm. Her butt was warm, and it felt delicious against the soft blanket wrapped around her. Her skirt was bunched up around her waist.

Rex Kyle. She hadn't thought about him in years. Time had done him justice. He was taller and fuller and...dominant. He was more slender than Samson and Nile, but his uniqueness attracted her to him all the same.

As she thought back on the few times she'd spent with him in high school, she acknowledged his nerdy side had been attractive even then, probably because of his confidence. He was smart. He knew it. He didn't apologize or hide the fact.

Charlotte suddenly wished Nile had been able to accompany her tonight. If he'd been present, he might have let her orgasm. Her pussy was still pulsing with the need, though it had subsided enough for her to relax her tense thighs.

She knew she was insatiable. Both her Masters knew it.

That's why she had two. They had an arrangement. An agreement. Their penthouse was large enough to give everyone space but still afforded them the ability to exercise their preferred fetish. It worked for them. Didn't it? When was the last time the three of them had sat down and taken one another's pulses? They used to do it frequently. They hadn't in a while. It wasn't any one person's fault. At least she didn't think it was.

And yet, here she was, receiving aftercare from another man. A man who'd come close to bringing her to orgasm. Maybe it was a coincidence. Maybe she needed to open her eyes.

Charlotte was well aware that most people wouldn't understand her living arrangement. It was unconventional. It was no one's business. No one in the fetish world would ever lift a brow, but vanilla folks were another story.

"You okay?" Rex asked in a deep tone that vibrated through her. He was running his fingers through her hair over and over, and she liked how it calmed her.

"Yes, Sir." She rolled onto her back, her head still on his lap, so she could look up at him. His brows were drawn together. She couldn't blame him for being confused. How many submissives would intentionally cut off a scene to avoid orgasm? What he didn't know was that she was under the control of two Doms. She didn't make her own choices when it came to playing, especially when they weren't present.

She liked Rex. He was different. Where Samson was all firmness and serious and discipline, while Nile was all about plans and organization and tidiness, Rex was something else. She held his gaze, trying to read him. He was caring. She could tell by the way he stroked her hair, how he had carefully explored the skin of her butt before he started his scene.

Yeah, Rex was touchy feely, concerned, nurturing.

Charlotte wanted to crawl up into his lap and set her head

on his shoulder. She wanted him to continue touching her everywhere. She wouldn't because she didn't have permission to even think such thoughts.

Not that Samson and Nile didn't let her play with others. They did. All she needed was permission. If she wanted to see Rex again, she would have to tell them about him and request another scene. If she wanted to orgasm under his control, she would have to include at least one of them in the scene.

This idea wasn't out of the realm of possibility. Nile would be arriving tomorrow at noon. He could accompany her to Club Zodiac tomorrow night. Perhaps if she asked nicely, he would grant her permission to play with Rex again.

There was a small glitch in this plan. There always was. She would have to explain her situation to Rex. It was her job to make sure anyone she did more than a cursory scene with outside of her family unit was fully informed and didn't mind the supervision she would submit to from Nile or Samson or both. She closed her eyes. Were they a family? She'd thought so. She'd been with them long enough to grow complacent. Or maybe all of them had.

"How long are you in town?" Rex asked.

She met his gaze again. "A few more days, Sir."

"Zodiac is open tomorrow night too. Will you be here?"

She swallowed over the lump in her throat. "Probably, Sir." *But not alone.*

He narrowed his gaze. "There is a *but* in your answer."

She shrugged, not wanting to have this conversation here. Not tonight. Not while she was still squirming from the need to come. "Are you free tomorrow morning, Sir? We could meet for coffee."

He nodded slowly, trying to read her. "I can do that. There's a nice place not far from here. I'll text you the address."

"Perfect. I should probably go. It's late. I've had a long day."

He helped her to her feet. "Do you have clothes to change into? It's going to be much colder outside than when you got here."

"Yes, Sir. I have a bag in the locker room."

He stood as he spoke, his hand cupping her cheek. "Good. I'll meet you at the entrance when you come out and give you my number."

She tipped her face into his touch, loving the feel of his fingers against her skin. The soft pads of his fingertips stroked her cheek. These were hands that spent all their time clicking on computer keyboards, not working with barbells or chopping vegetables. Soft. Gentle. Nurturing.

"How was your evening?" Samson asked when he called early the next morning. He was in his SUV, driving to the gym. "Did you behave?"

He chuckled. He knew her well. Behaving wasn't always one of her strong suits. Mostly because she enjoyed his punishments.

"I did, but it wasn't easy," she informed him. She was still snuggled in bed, burrowed under the covers. Charlotte was not a morning person. Never had been. Lucky for her, her three stores opened at ten. Not so early that she needed to be up and running before the sun.

Samson, on the other hand, often got to the gym before it opened at five am. Not every day, but frequently. His gym could run itself. He had plenty of qualified employees. But Samson was very involved in his business, hands on. She couldn't blame him. She visited all three of her boutiques nearly every day also, keeping tabs on everything. Just in case.

Nile ran a tight ship too. The reason he hadn't been able to get away to join her in Denver last night because he'd had an event he wanted to keep a close eye on to ensure the customer was happy. It had been a wealthy client, one Nile hoped to dazzle enough to get return business and glowing recommendations.

"I hear a story in your voice," Samson responded.

She spoke to him freely. This was part of their arrangement. When she was at home, she submitted unconditionally. When she was not, she spoke more freely. Not that she ever had permission to be disrespectful, but she often didn't address either man as Sir, especially in public. There were times they called a mutual break from their agreement inside the house too. They would sit around the dining room table, not touching each other, and visit any topic one of them needed resolved. It had been too long since they'd done that. "Yes. Turns out I knew the man Master Colin arranged for me to scene with last night. We went to high school together."

"Ah. Did you date him in high school?"

"No. Nothing like that. We just knew each other." She rolled onto her back, staring into the darkness. The blinds were still drawn tight. "He was the rocket scientist type. Still is. Apparently, he's also a Dom."

"How did the scene go?"

"A bit too well. He's an excellent flogger. I had to stop him when I realized I might orgasm."

Samson chuckled in her ear. "My insatiable little sub. He must have been good."

"He was, Sir." She slid that term of respect in because it felt right. Samson's response concerned her. He sounded blasé about her evening, while it had been eye-opening to her.

"Let me guess. You'd like to scene with him again tonight?"

"Yes, Sir."

"Give me a sec. I'm at the gym now. Let me switch off Bluetooth." After a few moments, Samson was back, his voice clearer without the sounds of the car. "I'll speak to Nile. He's on his way to the airport."

"Thank you, Sir."

"You're welcome. Honesty from each of us is what holds this together. You realize that, right?"

"Yes, Sir." She'd always considered herself damn lucky. She had two amazing Doms who doted on her and cared deeply for her. Their agreement didn't include total exclusion so much as complete disclosure. But something was off, and she wasn't about to point it out over the phone.

"We both know how much you enjoy submitting and how much you like to have sex. Keep this line of communication open, and you'll have everything you need."

Was she overthinking? Samson sounded normal. He was saying the right things. Words about communication, her needs, submitting. All of that was spot on.

"Yes, Sir. Oh, I'm meeting him for coffee this morning."

"Good. You explain your arrangement to him. See how he feels. I'll speak to Nile. And, Charlotte?"

"Yes, Sir."

"I'm proud of you."

"Thank you, Sir."

She actually felt a bit choked up as she ended the call. It was early still. She could take her time getting ready. She wished she'd asked for permission to use her vibrator this morning to take the edge off before she showered, but considering Samson was on his way into the gym and Nile was heading to the airport, she didn't think it would be appropriate to plead with either of them to grant her an orgasm. So, she closed her eyes and breathed through the desire, focusing on what she was going to say to Rex in a few hours.

Charlotte hadn't found herself in this situation often, but it had occurred a handful of times in the past few years. Either she or one of her Masters would introduce a fourth person into their play, negotiations would ensue, and then she would find herself submitting to another Dom or Domme for an evening. So far, nothing more had come of any of the times they'd brought in an outsider, but none of the three of them was closed to the option of including other people.

Since Charlotte was the one who found Rex and knew him, it was her responsibility to meet with him and negotiate. Or at least fill him in. She doubted in the end her opinion about what sort of arrangement she might have with him would hold much weight.

She grinned into the darkness, deciding to drag herself out of bed and get in the shower.

CHAPTER 5

Charlotte glanced around at the festive atmosphere of the crowded coffee shop as she opened the front door. With Christmas just three weeks away, the store had red and green sparkly garland draped across each wall, bells above the doorway, and twinkling lights around the cash register.

Lucky for her, she enjoyed the holidays, because her three stores were similarly decked out. The soft sounds of pop Christmas songs filtered through the background, audible just barely over the chatter of patrons.

Charlotte scanned the room, spotting Rex as he stood from a table in the back corner, waving her direction. His body language was oddly stiffer than last night. She made her way between the patrons and their packages, smiling as she realized it was a Saturday morning. Most people had been out shopping for gifts already.

When she reached him, he pulled out a chair and slid it back in as she lowered onto it. She shrugged out of her coat and draped it over the chair.

"You look great. Did you sleep well?" he asked.

He didn't return to his seat. Instead, he was standing next

to her, tugging the bottom of his sweater down. Nervous? Where was the confident man who'd flogged her last night? This version of Rex was more like the guy she remembered from high school.

She smiled at him, wondering if he perhaps became a different person when he stepped into Zodiac. It wasn't unheard of.

"I did. Thank you."

"I'll go order you something. What do you like?"

"A latte would be great. It's cold out there." She shivered as she rubbed her arms.

"Muffin? Croissant? Danish?"

"Whatever looks good."

He nodded and weaved his way through the crowd toward the barista.

She watched his retreat, enjoying the view of his ass encased in dark jeans today. He wore a brown knit sweater and had a brown plaid scarf around his neck. He moved with less confidence than last night, and she noted he shuffled his weight from side to side as he waited his turn, and then leaned over the counter to speak, pointing at something in the display case.

She was still watching him as he returned with a steaming cup in one hand and a plate in the other. He set both in front of her. "Sugar?"

"Nope. This is perfect. Thank you."

Sitting on the plate was a muffin she guessed to be pumpkin.

He slid back into the seat across from her at the small table, his knee bumping hers.

"Did you eat?" she asked.

"Yes. I enjoyed that same muffin actually. That's how I know it's a good choice."

She pinched off a bite and popped it into her mouth,

moaning as it melted onto her tongue. "You can never go wrong with pumpkin at this time of year. It's guaranteed to be fresh."

He stared at her mouth as she licked a crumb from the corner, his hands resting on the table, clasped together, thumbs moving.

A shiver raced up her spine. He was interested in her. There was no doubt. The way he sat so close, his knee touching hers, his stance open. His other knee was bouncing slightly. He was nervous. It was cute.

She really needed to tell him a few things before she got accused of leading him on. She took a sip of her latte and set the cup back down. "Listen, I, uh, need to tell you a few things."

"I assume that's why we're here." He swallowed, forcing a half smile. He was worried. He handed her a napkin like a gentleman though.

"You're right."

"Let me guess. You're in a relationship with someone in Seattle. It would explain your hesitation last night."

Her face flushed. "Sort of. I mean yes. I'm definitely in a relationship, but it's a negotiated D/s arrangement." She paused before adding the next part. "With two men actually."

He nodded slowly, carefully schooling his reaction. Or perhaps she simply hadn't surprised him. "Did you set the terms for last night's scene yourself? Or did one of them?"

She smiled. He was astute. "They did."

Rex leaned back, rubbing his chin. "So, let me get this straight. You're in a relationship with two people at the same time, and they permitted you to go to Club Zodiac while you're in Denver, but they called ahead and dictated exactly what you were allowed to do."

"That's exactly it." Charlotte shouldn't have been surprised that he put all the pieces together so quickly and so accurately. He was fucking intelligent.

"Huh. Interesting." He nodded slowly. "You've surprised me. I didn't think anyone could shock me."

She pinched off another bite of muffin. "You don't look that surprised to be honest."

He shrugged. "I've been involved in the lifestyle for many years. I've seen every kind of relationship. I would never judge anyone for how they choose to live. It's not that. It's that I know you, at least I used to. I just wouldn't have pictured you in a BDSM triad." He held up both hands, palms out. "Again, not judging. Not at all. Just absorbing."

She ate another bite and took a sip of her latte, letting him ponder her announcement. It was a lot to absorb even if you were in the lifestyle.

He finally leaned forward, putting his elbows on the table and stroking his chin again, his face closer to hers. "Why did these two Doms of yours give you permission to come to the club at all? Or why not come with you to Denver?" He narrowed his gaze. "I'm trying to imagine even letting you out of the house to go to the store if you were mine and willing to give me that kind of control." His grin told her he was half teasing.

She smiled. "It's complicated. I work hard at my day job. When I'm done working, I like to flip a switch and turn over control to someone else. I've known that for years. It's not a twenty-four seven thing for me because I'm driven during the day. It's all the other hours. I thrive on the dominance. Even when it's from afar."

He held her gaze, listening intently, rubbing his hands on his thighs.

She glanced around, ensuring what she already knew—that the place was too crowded and too loud for anyone to overhear them. "When I walk in the front door of our home, I'm theirs. I belong to whichever one of them is home."

He cocked his head. "You all three live together?"

"Yes."

"Got it. Go ahead."

"We have an agreement. I obey them in everything. I've never broken that trust. I like to play. A lot. So much so that even when I'm not specifically with one or both of them, I get immense pleasure from doing as they instruct. Like last night. They were both in Seattle, but they were dominating me like a puppet from afar."

"Makes sense."

"Nile meant to come with me, but he had to work last night at the last minute. He's on his way here now. He'll join me tonight. You can meet him. If you'd like."

Rex held her gaze. He nodded again. "I'd like that." He tapped his fingers on the small table. "Do your Doms know Colin? How did they arrange the scene?"

"Yes. Nile owns a catering business. He did a job for Colin recently in Seattle. They apparently got to know each other. Nile arranged my scene. He's extremely organized. It was a coincidence you and I knew each other of course."

"Did you speak to them after our scene?"

"Yes. I always do. We don't have secrets." She felt her face heat, which would be obvious to anyone, considering how pale her skin was. She was telling the truth. They didn't keep secrets. But had they been omitting things lately? "I told Samson I had to stop our scene because I got too close to orgasm," she admitted. Even speaking those words again now made her squirm in her seat. It was her turn to be nervous. She shifted her weight from side to side, remembering how turned on she'd been less than twelve hours ago while the man sitting across from her flogged her expertly.

Rex leaned back again, blowing out a breath and running a hand through his hair. "Charlotte, what are we doing here?"

She bit her lower lip and then released it. "I was hoping you might be interested in doing a scene with Nile and me tonight."

Rex hesitated, his face frozen, not giving a single hint as to what he was thinking. Finally, he took a breath. "You want to scene with both of us?"

"Yes," she breathed, knowing she probably sounded anxious.

It was awkward having this conversation here in public. Safer, but awkward nonetheless. She found herself straddling the two worlds. This coffee wasn't meant to involve her submitting, but on the other hand, it was nearly impossible to discuss submission and the way she managed it without planting one foot on that side of the line.

"How long have you been with these two men?" Rex's eyes were drawn together skeptically. His hands were planted on his thighs but no longer moving. Gripping instead.

"I met Nile first. He catered my grand opening actually. Three years ago. I had been in Seattle a year at the time and had frequented a club there called Surrender. We recognized each other from the club. We said nothing that day, but the next time I was at Surrender, I did a scene with him. We started playing together regularly after that."

Charlotte paused to study Rex's face. He was watching her intently. Listening. "Go on."

She took a deep breath. "About six months later, I arrived at Surrender a few hours before Nile could get there. By that time, we were seeing each other outside of the club. Since I wasn't busy, another Dom, Samson, asked me to do a demo with him for a group of newer members."

"Did you previously know Samson?"

She nodded. "Yes. Peripherally. I hadn't done a scene with him, but we knew each other from coming to the club. I'd seen him perform many times. I didn't hesitate to do the demo." Another deep breath. "Anyway, he's nothing like Nile. He's bossy and authoritative and demanding. I was used to Nile's softer approach. He's more of the sensual type. Blindfolds and gentle touches. Ice cubes and strawberries." She shivered as thoughts raced through her mind.

Rex waved a hand through the air. "Got it."

"The demo was all about the nuances of spanking. I spent the next forty-five minutes bent over a bench wearing nothing but a thong and cropped tank top while Samson used my pale ass to teach a group of people how to cup their palms and where to strike and how hard to get a variety of results."

A slow smile spread across Rex's face as he watched her. "You're blushing."

She rubbed her cheeks with both hands. "Hazard of fair skin. This is nothing. You should have seen me that night. I had no idea I enjoyed pain before that day." She lowered her voice to barely above a whisper. "When Nile arrived, he found me nearly on my knees. I was so aroused, my legs were shaking. Instead of removing me from the crowd to see to me himself, he asked Samson to bring me to orgasm."

Rex nodded. "And the rest is history. A bit of yin and yang."

"Basically. All three of us recognized we had a dynamic together pretty quickly. Samson owns a gym in the city. He's older and more established than either of us. He has a penthouse. Nile and I went to his place the next night to explore a bit further in private. We hit it off, started spending the night on weekends, and eventually both Nile and I moved in with Samson."

"Wow. That's a lot." Rex scooted his cup out of the way and leaned forward again. "Committed but not exclusive?"

She drew in a deep breath. "We don't have sex outside of our group without permission. We also don't do anything without checking in with the others first."

"So, if Nile had been present, he would have given you permission to orgasm last night?"

A hand landed on Charlotte's shoulder and eased up to cup her neck.

She jerked in her seat, twisting around to lift her gaze, finding Nile leaning over her shoulder. He kissed her cheek and then leaned farther, making eye contact with Rex. "The answer to your question is *yes*. And I can't wait to learn more about the Dom who got my little sub so hot and bothered she had to stop the scene." He slid casually into the vacant chair next to Charlotte, hand still possessively wrapped around her neck.

Rex lifted both brows and then reached out with a hand. "Rex Kyle."

Nile took his hand in a firm shake. "Nile Ellis. Nice to meet you."

"How did you...?" Charlotte asked, rolling her eyes at Nile. "Never mind. You'd find me if I were at the bottom of the ocean."

He slid his hand to her chin and cupped it a bit firmer than usual. "You know it. And the eye rolling won't go unpunished either."

She stiffened, rubbing her palms on her thighs. Luckily her legs weren't bare. It was too cold out for that. She was wearing black tights and short black stylish boots under a black skirt this morning. Her thick cable knit sweater was a deep maroon.

Nile leaned closer once more, this time kissing the tip of her nose. "What'd I miss?" He shifted his gaze toward Rex.

Rex stared at Nile, uncertainty about this entire thing written on his face. Charlotte couldn't blame him. She suddenly felt horrible for even considering asking him to play with her and Nile. He was obviously interested in her, and she was asking too much from him. "Charlotte was just telling me about your arrangement."

Nile slapped both hands on his thighs, still leaning into her but not quite as possessively. "We aren't conventional. That's for sure. I'm sorry I wasn't there last night. I enjoy watching Charlotte's skin pinken."

Charlotte finished off her coffee and set it aside. "You do realize my skin could get just as pink under your own palm, right?" she joked.

Nile loved to watch. He did not enjoy swatting her though.

"Nope. Wouldn't be the same. Then I'd have to concentrate on your ass instead of your face. I prefer to watch your mouth fall open, your eyes roll back, and your neck elongate as you get off from the contact." He winked at her.

Rex chuckled. "That is one of the unfortunate parts I miss out on when I'm the one wielding the floggers. I glance from time to time at my submissive's face to see where she is emotionally, but I can't let my dick get involved, or someone could get hurt."

This frank conversation with a man Charlotte hardly knew and Nile had never met was slightly awkward. Charlotte glanced around, once again assuring no one was paying attention to the three of them. She doubted anyone else in the room was discussing the merits of watching a woman get spanked.

"I can't wait to see you in action," Nile told Rex. "That is if you don't mind."

"Of course not. I'm used to having a bit of an audience. I don't mind the intrusion at all. I also have no problem with you speaking to Charlotte while I work. Top her all you want. As long as you don't direct me, we'll be fine."

Charlotte sat up straighter at Rex's words. Damn. He was

going to do this. When it came down to it, he was all Dom as soon as he walked into the club. Same as Nile and Samson. Perhaps a different sort of Dom, but not one who bottomed for anyone.

"We have a deal." Nile smiled at both of them.

CHAPTER 6

As Charlotte and Nile left the coffee shop, he pulled her in close to his side and kissed her temple. "Shopping?"

"Sounds great." She flattened her gloved hand on his waist and took in deep breaths of the crisp winter air. "While we have the opportunity, let's stop and get something for Samson. He's so hard to buy for."

"That's for sure. You're the easiest. Jewelry, lingerie, fuzzy cuffs..." He laughed at his last addition.

She giggled. "You're easy too. Pots, pans, feathers..."

He laughed at that one. "What do we get a man who doesn't cook or tease?"

She tipped her head back. "Well, I'm certainly not buying him a whip, paddle, or flogger. He doesn't need any new ideas." Or maybe he did need new ideas. But she wasn't going to provide them for him. What was the fun in that?

Nile slid his hand into hers and gave her a tug. "Come on. Let's pop into a sports store and see if we can get inspired."

She skipped alongside him to keep up once he got excited, and a few minutes later, they stepped into the warmth of a three-story sporting goods store. Like every other place on earth, Christmas music was playing through the speaker system and garland was draped over nearly every display rack. "He could use a new sports bag to take back and forth to the gym. The one he's been using has a broken zipper on the side pocket."

"Excellent idea." Nile removed her gloves and tucked them into his pockets, threading her fingers with his as they wandered through the store.

She loved the way he kept her close at all times. The little touches, like pocketing her gloves, tucking her hair back after she pulled her hood off, guiding her between the people and racks. He did all this naturally without thinking. He always had.

When he stopped to flip through a rack of shirts, she watched his profile, absorbing the fact that he didn't release her. His attention might have been focused on price tags and sizes, but she was never an afterthought. Not for a second. She needed to remember that, but she couldn't seem to shake her fears. Maybe it was all the weird emotions around the holidays. She released a breath and squeezed his hand.

She adored this man. Anyone who passed by them would think they were a regular everyday couple. And in some respects, they were, except that another man also slept in her bed most nights. Oh, and she'd almost had an orgasm last night at the hands of a third man.

Charlotte was worried about herself. She was also worried about her committed relationship with Nile and Samson. It seemed incongruent that they were as eager and willing to accommodate her as they were, to encourage her to meet Rex for coffee and arrange to play with him tonight.

Now, Nile was perfectly normal. He glanced at her, his brows drawing together. "You okay?"

She nodded, lying. *No. I'm not. I need to talk to you. Both of you. I'm confused and worried and nervous.* She wouldn't, of course. Not here. Not when Samson was in Seattle and she and Nile were in Denver.

The issues she was concerned about didn't really have anything to do with Rex. He was just the catalyst, reminding her that she and Nile and Samson had gotten complacent.

It bothered her that Rex was on her mind while she was wandering around with Nile. She thought about how nervous Rex had been that morning, how he'd been flustered and stressed meeting her at the coffee shop. It had been cute and endearing in a way, an interesting side of him that matched more accurately with the guy in her physics class.

At the club, Rex was all Dom, on his game. Outside, he was less confident.

God, why the hell do I keep thinking about Rex?

She shook him from her mind and leaned into Nile, loving the scent of him. She wrapped her arm around his, entwining herself with him.

Nile led her through the racks until they came to the gym bags. "Lord, there are ten thousand. How will we choose?"

She released him to wander slowly up and down the aisle. "I think he likes to have a shoulder strap, and a side pocket to hold his power drink, one deep enough that it won't slide out." She picked up a black bag after a few minutes and turned to show it to Nile.

Nile was watching her, and she suddenly realized he had been this entire time. He reached out, snagged her around the waist, and hauled her against him, front to front.

The breath whooshed out of her lungs.

He cupped her face with his other hand, searching her eyes. His expression was serious. His thumb grazed her bottom lip. "You're so gorgeous when you're focused."

She flushed.

He closed the last few inches and kissed her lips gently. "That bag is perfect. Let's go back to the hotel."

She smiled. "Will you make it worth my while, Sir?"

He wiggled his brows. "Maybe I just want to see you naked."

She sighed dramatically. "What if I want to see *you* naked?"

He tapped her nose with one finger. "You're not in charge, though, are you?"

Nope. And that's how she liked it.

Nile led her through the store, heading for the check out. Five minutes later they were back on the sidewalk.

"I think we might want to get Samson more than just a sports bag for Christmas," she pointed out.

"Yep, but not today." He grinned at her. "I'm feeling the urge to dominate someone."

"Anyone in particular?" she teased.

"Definitely."

~

"Are you sure about this, Sir?" Charlotte asked three hours later. She was lounging on the king-sized bed in her hotel room. Nile sat in the chair across from her. Samson was on the speakerphone on the mattress between them.

She was wearing a short silk robe, of course. Being out of town did not mean bending the rules. This hotel was currently their home away from home. As soon as they'd entered the room, she had removed everything, folded her clothes up by the door, and put on a robe.

She'd expected Nile to dominate her using any of a number of his favorite methods. Instead, he'd sat back and watched her moving around in her robe, indicating she should return the call she'd missed from her realtor. So, she'd spent the next hour on the phone discussing the negotiations for the property she'd looked at.

So far, Nile still hadn't touched her. He'd been sitting on

the chair across the room, feet on the coffee table, laptop open on his thighs. His face had been intent as he worked. She knew there were a few events his people were covering while he was out of town.

And then Samson had called, and here they were. Charlotte was biting her lower lip. It had been a while since they'd invited a fourth person into their world. She was a bit worried about how their interaction with Rex might go later that night. Rex had verbally seemed on board, but she got the sense he was uncertain.

Samson chuckled through the line. "She's smitten, isn't she, Nile?"

"Yep." Nile leaned forward, putting his elbows on his knees.

Charlotte was unnerved at the way they were discussing her feelings. Or maybe she was unnerved for having those feelings. The truth was, she couldn't wait to have Rex's flogger on her again. Nor could she wait to orgasm for him.

Maybe the reason her body was alight with need had more to do with the fact that she hadn't come since leaving the house yesterday. Nope. Not even then. She hadn't had an orgasm since earlier in the morning before leaving for work yesterday.

She squirmed, and then attempted to mask her need by rolling onto her belly and stretching out on the bed, propping her chin up with her palm as she resumed staring at the phone.

When she flicked her gaze to Nile, she found his brows were high, and he was smirking. He knew she was needy. Neither of them usually required her to go so long without an orgasm unless she was being punished. Granted, she had broken the rules the afternoon before, but that discipline was over. Today was a new day. It was afternoon. She'd been with

Nile for half the day. She'd been nearly naked in this hotel room for three hours. She was horny.

"Nile, would you put me on FaceTime please." Samson's voice was calm and precise.

Nile reached across the bed, swiped the phone up, and tapped the screen. Seconds later, he moved to sit on the edge of the mattress, holding the phone out in a way that both of them were on the screen.

Samson looked amazing. He was wearing his usual gym clothes but he was sitting at his desk in his home office. She had always loved the incongruency of his amazing body out of place in the room with the mahogany furniture and leather chair. He leaned back, crossing one ankle over the opposite knee. He must have had the phone propped on the desk. "Nile, please tell me more about Rex."

Charlotte swallowed. She wasn't sure how she felt about this situation yet herself, let alone having these two men who she belonged to dissecting it.

Nile spoke, his gaze on Charlotte. "He's fucking smart. I can tell you that. He works for a hacking service. He's a computer genius. You'd think he would be nerdy, but he's dominant enough to make that side of him seem sexy. At least I presume, considering how he made Charlotte squirm while we were at coffee."

Charlotte flinched. She wasn't sure how she felt about how flippantly they were discussing Rex. Like it didn't matter at all that she'd scened with another man. The way Samson laughed and said she was smitten unnerved her. Did either of them even care that she'd gotten so aroused last night that she'd almost come? On top of that, she felt confident her scene with Rex meant more to him than it should have. She feared they were taking advantage of Rex by setting up a repeat performance for tonight.

"Do me a favor, sweetheart," Samson said. "Please turn

over. Take off your robe. Prop yourself against the pillows at the headboard. Legs spread."

Charlotte inhaled deeply, shaking her wandering thoughts from her mind. She was here now, in the hotel room, Nile by her side, Samson dominating her through the phone. That meant everything.

She rolled over and did as he asked, parting her knees wide, knowing Nile would adjust the phone to include her nudity.

"Wider, Charlotte. Pull your labia apart for me." Samson's voice had slipped into his authoritative dominant self—not that he often had another voice.

She did as requested, trying not to shake. No matter how long they'd been together, it still unnerved her to perform for them on FaceTime. She'd done so dozens of times, and it made her undeniably horny, but it was almost a stretch for her.

"Is she wet?" Samson asked unnecessarily.

"Very," Nile responded.

"If I were there, would she be over my knee right now?"

"Yes. You should have seen the eye roll I got from her in front of Rex." Nile smiled.

Charlotte wanted to throw a pillow at him.

Samson continued. "Tsk. Too bad you don't enjoy spanking her. I'd swat her pussy right this second and leave her squirming if I could."

"I'll be happy to have Rex punish her later if you'd like."

Samson smiled wider. "Excellent plan."

Charlotte shuddered, feeling them gang up on her. If she were another woman, she would run from the room. But she wasn't. She loved the dominance. She loved the difference they each provided. She even loved the fact that Rex was yet another sort of Dom.

"Let go of your pussy and play with your tits for me, sweetheart."

Charlotte released her lower lips and smoothed her hands up to stroke her breasts. Her nipples puckered immediately.

"Pinch them," Nile added. "I know it's hard for Samson to see the tips very well, but I can. I want them swollen and sensitive."

Charlotte bit into her lower lip as she gripped her nipples between her fingers and thumbs and drew them away from her breasts. She gasped and her knees started shaking.

"Would you bring the camera in closer, Nile?"

Nile slid farther up the bed, the phone jiggling in his hand for a moment before he brought it slowly toward her pussy, hovering for a moment between her legs and then easing it up her body, featuring first her sex and then a breast.

"Nice," Samson stated. "Maybe let her play like that for a while, but don't let her get off. Set a timer for thirty minutes. That's from me. After her time is up, you decide what she deserves. I hope you packed something sexy for tonight. I wish I could be there. I'll be waiting for the details in the morning."

"Sorry you're going to miss the action. I'll have her give you a play by play after."

"Can't wait. Be safe. Talk to you later."

"Bye, Sir," Charlotte murmured, finding it difficult to focus while she pinched her nipples.

Nile ended the connection and set the phone on the bedside table. He then proceeded to prop himself on his side, his cheek against his palm, his face six inches from her pussy.

Charlotte closed her eyes as she circled her nipples with her finger tips, keeping them erect without torturing them. She knew the object here was for her to remain aroused for half an hour without coming. It was going to be a challenge with Nile staring at her. She couldn't continue to pinch without coming. Instead, she alternated between stroking her swollen globes, circling the tips, and tapping them. Each time she reached that part, she sucked in a breath.

"My girl is so very aroused right now," Nile whispered after a while. "I bet you'd like me to lean in close and flick my tongue over your clit."

She moaned, letting her head roll to one side. He knew exactly what he was doing. She had no idea how much time had passed, but she figured not long yet. This was going to get so much worse.

"Leave your tits alone for a while. Slide your hands down and hold your folds open for me."

She gritted her teeth as she obeyed that order. Since Nile wasn't the sort of Dom who enjoyed striking his submissive, he typically left the discipline to Samson. But when denial was the method of punishment, he could easily get on board.

"Good girl. Stroke a finger through your folds and circle your clit. Slowly."

He was pushing her limits. She was hanging on by a thread. If he asked her to touch her clit, she would be in serious trouble. "Sir..." she warned as she dragged the tip of her finger through her wetness.

"I know, baby. I can see you're struggling. Wide circles. Don't touch your clit. It's so pink and swollen right now. Gorgeous."

She didn't even need to hold the hood back. Her nub was exposed on its own. She circled the tip several times, painstakingly slowly, the fingers of her other hand still holding her folds open. The worst part was feeling Nile's breath every time it hit her sensitive skin. Warm. Sexy. Maddening.

"That's my girl. Switch back to your nipples now. Keep them hard for me. I love how the tips stiffen when you stroke them."

She let her knees fall open wider as she did his bidding. He had her switch back and forth several times before finally grabbing her wrists and hauling them over her head. "You did good, baby. Where's that vibrator you packed?"

Thank. God.

She could barely speak. "In my suitcase," she murmured. "Purple toiletry bag."

He kissed her briefly and then released her to pad across the room. Moments later, he was back, the thick, curved, vibrator in his hand. He resumed his spot between her legs and stroked the tip of the phallus along her thigh. "If you can stay still, keeping your hands above your head and your legs open for me, I'll give you the relief you need."

"Yes, Sir." She would do anything to be granted an orgasm, and she knew Nile would give her relief. However, he would do it on his timeline, not hers.

She focused on remaining still while he dragged the tip of the vibrator along the sensitive skin between her pussy and her thigh, touching nothing. She was so wet. So needy. Desperate.

She fisted the pillow behind her head as he inched closer and finally slid the phallus into her tight channel. She moaned when he angled it so that it pressed against the top of her sheath as he pulled it partway out. Without removing the vibrator, he turned it on. The lowest setting was more than she would need to come. She prayed he didn't intend to insist she not come or that he wouldn't drag this out very long.

"Right there," he stated as he jiggled the head of the vibrator against her G-spot. "That's all you need, isn't it, baby?"

"Yes, Sir," she whispered, fighting against the orgasm.

Nile centered the tip on just the right spot and pressed upward. "Go ahead. Come for me, Charlotte."

She did exactly that without hesitation, letting her pent-up need go less than a second later. Her body shook as she pulsed around the vibrator. She hadn't gotten any contact with her clit, but she hadn't needed it. Not this time.

When she was fully spent, he removed the vibrator, turned it off, and set it aside, his lips coming to her inner thigh to nibble a path toward her pussy. "You're so sexy, Charlotte. I'm one of the luckiest men alive."

CHAPTER 7

Rex was waiting at the bar when Nile approached him later that night at Club Zodiac. Small talk between the two men lacked the awkwardness he would have expected. Obviously, Nile was secure in his claim on Charlotte. Secure enough to share her with other Doms.

It wasn't unheard of. There were plenty of people who came to Zodiac with their significant others and then parted ways to play with other people. Rex had dominated many men and women whose partners were either engaged in another scene, watching, or not even available that evening.

Rex had told himself over and over throughout the day that this situation was no different from any other, but he also knew he was lying to himself. It *was* different. If for no other reason than the fact that his dick had been hard all day and his mind had wandered so badly he hadn't been able to concentrate on a single thing.

He spent a few minutes with Nile focusing on their intentions for the evening, combining their goals. It gave Rex some time to center himself while Charlotte changed clothes in the locker room. He hadn't seen her yet, but the moment she stepped into view, his breath left his lungs.

Now that Charlotte was approaching, he knew for certain he had a problem. He wanted her. And she was not his. Nor did she live in Denver. Nor was she available at all. She had not one, but two Doms. They obviously adored her and took good care of her.

And yet.

Yeah, his dick was hard.

Charlotte wore a white chiffon shift. It left nothing to the imagination. It was held up by tiny spaghetti straps and gathered under her breasts before flaring out like a cloud, reaching just below her bottom. The lace that covered her breasts was denser than the bodice, but not enough to completely hide her pink nipples. A matching thong rounded out the outfit, teasing anyone she passed.

As she approached, head bowed, hands clasped behind her back, Rex took several more deep breaths.

"She is a sight to behold, isn't she?" Nile asked from his side.

"That's an understatement. You're a lucky man." There was no reason to hide his attraction. He wouldn't be able to anyway. Why lie?

Nile clapped a hand on Rex's shoulder. "I share nicely when it's called for," he stated loud enough for Charlotte to hear.

Damn, this relationship was complicated. Rex was slightly unnerved. He didn't feel like sharing. He felt like having Charlotte for himself.

"You look delicious, baby," Nile stated when she stepped into his space. He tucked her hair behind her ear and leaned in to kiss her cheek. "I can't wait to see your skin pinkened against this white material. Since I couldn't see evidence you'd been flogged last night by the time I was able to examine your bottom, I asked Rex to use something not quite as soft tonight. I assume you don't mind?"

"No, Sir." Her voice was solid. She wasn't just humoring him. If she'd simply nodded or given a weaker consent, Rex wouldn't have been comfortable with the arrangement.

"We're both going to play with you, baby. Combine our skills."

She visibly shivered, making Rex smile. He had no hesitation about how the two of them were going to dominate her. His only concern was falling for her more every moment. That was a risk.

Rex dominated lots of people every month. Several a night when he came to Zodiac, but he rarely found himself wanting more from them. And never did he get as hung up as he already was with Charlotte. *Who is taken.*

Suddenly, Colin stepped around the corner. "Hey." He extended a hand toward Nile. "You made it. Charlotte told me you were coming this morning. I'm glad you made time to come to the club tonight."

Nile nodded. "Sounds like my little submissive had a good time. I figured I better see what all the fuss was about." He winked at Rex.

Colin chuckled as he shook Rex's hand next, still speaking to Nile. "Rex is the best flogger I know. I watched him with Charlotte. He definitely got to her."

"That's what I hear." Nile wrapped an arm around Charlotte's waist and tugged her closer. "You may speak freely."

Charlotte lifted her gaze toward Colin. "Nice to see you again, Sir. Thank you for having us."

"You're welcome. Please, anytime you're in Denver, feel free to visit us."

Charlotte smiled.

Rex loved how her face lit up when she was pleased. He'd seen it several times so far, especially while they were having coffee that morning.

"Did you reserve something for these folks for tonight?" Colin asked Rex.

"I did. I'm joining them in fact."

Nile nodded. "I'm not much of a masochist myself, but I do enjoy watching someone else take a palm or a flogger to Charlotte's pale skin."

Colin tipped his head in agreement. "Can't disagree with you there. Her skin is amazing. Several people gathered to watch last night. If you're planning to reenact that scene, I'm sure you'll draw a crowd, my own submissive included."

"I'm glad you found her enjoyable. We'll be operating with different parameters tonight." Nile slid a hand up to cup Charlotte's cheek. "You ready to perform, baby?"

She turned a lovely shade of red that anyone could discern even in the dim lighting. "Yes, Sir."

Rex wanted to cup that cheek himself, and he had to shake thoughts of sliding his hands up and down her entire body from his head and get straightened out before they started this scene.

She's not yours, he reminded himself—a mantra he realized he was going to have to repeat several times in the next hour.

Charlotte resumed her submissive stance the moment Colin left them.

Rex led the way to the St. Andrew's Cross he had booked their time on. Instead of addressing Charlotte, Rex spoke to Nile. "Restraints?"

Nile smiled broadly. "Now you're speaking my language."

Rex pulled a set of black Velcro ankle and wrist cuffs out of his bag and held them up to show Nile. He watched as Nile led Charlotte to the cross and then threaded his hand in her hair and pulled her against his chest, his lips landing on her ear.

She nodded several times at whatever he told her. When she was permitted to step back, she lifted her arms in the air.

Rex's breath caught again as Nile eased the thin garment over her head. Her breasts were amazing. The perfect size for her body, pert, full, creamy white. Her nipples were a deep pink.

Nile cupped the globes and thumbed the tips.

She arched into him, her head tipping back, making Nile smile.

He released her abruptly and rounded to her back to gather her gorgeous wavy hair into his palms. He worked his fingers through it several times and then stepped to the side and braided the thick tresses off one shoulder so that the final braid hung over her chest instead of down her back. It would keep any strands from getting snagged by his flogger.

Leaving her thong in place, Nile guided her to face the cross before stepping up behind her and lifting her hands up in a V above her head. He adjusted the pegs, lowering them to accommodate her height, and then she wrapped her fingers around the wooden dowels.

Rex couldn't tear his gaze away as Nile smoothed his hands down her arms and then paused to cup her breasts, pressing his chest against her naked back. He toyed with her nipples until she moaned, whispering in her ear as he made her shiver.

One last word from him made her still, but her mouth dropped open and her head tipped back against his shoulder. She clearly struggled to avoid squirming as Nile continued to thrum her nipples.

Finally, he released her, kissed her shoulder, and then stepped back. When he turned around to face Rex, he reached out a hand.

For a moment, Rex wasn't sure what Nile intended by the gesture, and then he remembered he was holding the restraints. He lifted them toward Nile, who took them and returned to Charlotte's side. He was meticulous as he wrapped each cuff around her wrists and attached the other end above the pegs on the cross. Charlotte would still be able to hold on to the pegs with her fists, but she wouldn't be able to release them and jerk her arms down.

Her arms were pulled slightly tighter when Nile crouched at her side and tapped her leg, silently telling her to widen her stance.

She wasn't new to this apparatus. She set her feet apart in exactly the right spot that permitted Nile to secure her ankles to the bottom of the giant X. Her chest rose and fell as she leaned her forehead on one of the boards, taking deep cleansing breaths.

Rex had flogged dozens of people on this cross. He'd watched dozens more. None had been as glorious as Charlotte, and they hadn't even started. He forced himself to look away, shaking the intensity from his mind as he bent to grab his intended floggers from his bag. He needed to focus on the task at hand and stop lusting after the woman spread out in front of him.

The plan was to take turns working with her, alternating between flogging and teasing. Apparently, Nile was a more sensual sort of Dom who enjoyed tormenting his sub with bondage and light touches. While they'd waited for Charlotte to change, Nile had informed Rex that Samson was the disciplinarian of the two of them. He handled the spanking and any objects that induced pain.

Nile had smiled as he'd described how Samson would clamp her nipples and then Nile would sooth the offended tips with his tongue. It would seem the three of them had the perfect arrangement.

They certainly don't need you to step up and add anything.

As Rex gripped a pair of floggers, adjusting them in his hands, he watched Nile once again flatten his front to Charlotte's back, whispering in her ear, stroking up and down her sides, notably avoiding her tits.

A slight gasp made Rex turn his head to find that a crowd had gathered already. Some were aware that Rex was about to flog a submissive, but others were simply awed by the scene already in progress.

Nile finally stepped back and turned toward Rex. "She's ready. She's not allowed to come without permission, which I will occasionally grant her."

Rex lifted his brows. *More than once?*

Nile didn't notice or at least didn't respond.

Rex once again centered himself, closing his eyes for a moment to breathe deeply as he began to swish the floggers slowly through the air in a figure eight, adjusting to the feel of them in his palms before he would step closer to his submissive.

When he decided he was ready, he approached, concentrating on his target while forcing himself to ignore the appeal he had toward her. She was simply any other sub who wanted him to flog her. Nothing more.

He inched closer as he artistically waved the leather strands through the air so that when the tips first made contact with her shoulder blades, the touch would be nearly nonexistent.

Rex entered into his zone with ease, paying attention to two things at once—the swish of the floggers and the stance of the submissive. He would keep a close eye on her every reaction, as he always did, making sure she didn't stiffen or show signs of distress.

After working with her last night, Rex seriously doubted Charlotte would need him to back off at any time. For one, he now knew her tolerance level was higher than average. For another thing, she was calmer, knowing enough about him to anticipate his style.

He could do this. He was in his element. He just needed to ignore the fact that for the first time in years, he was interested in the submissive he was in charge of. After all, he reminded himself once again, *she is not yours.*

CHAPTER 8

Charlotte closed her eyes and relaxed her forehead against the cool wood, lightly gripping the rungs above her head. As the first tips of leather hit her shoulder blades, she released a long breath. To her, this was heaven. It was an even better level of heaven than usual since she had not one but two Doms at her back.

The floggers Rex had chosen for tonight were slightly denser and heavier than last night, but not harsh enough to worry her. She'd been flogged by worse. Besides, she knew Rex well enough after last night to realize he would take his time and he wasn't the sort of Dom who liked to inflict unnecessary pain.

As he gradually increased the pressure, he began to angle the contact so that it eased down her body until he reached her thighs and then centered once again on her butt.

God, it felt so good. She loved the way an accomplished Dom could zero in on her sensitive skin and apply just the right amount of pressure to drag her into subspace. Doubly awesome tonight was that Nile was watching, and he would make sure she had at least one amazing orgasm.

Sinking into the feelings, Charlotte was only peripherally aware of the gathering crowd. They were politely quiet. She didn't mind performing for people. Not at all. In fact, she liked to think others learned from her experiences.

In the early days she'd had trouble reaching orgasm in front of people. It had been difficult to concentrate while being watched by strangers. The first time she came during a scene at a club was with Nile before they met Samson. He had been new to Shibari at the time and spent almost an hour turning her into a work of art. By the time he was done, she was panting and desperate.

Nile had circled around her suspended body, stroking her skin, driving her need higher by the second. Finally, he blindfolded her and that was exactly what she needed. It allowed her to lose herself in her mind, pretend they were alone, focus on nothing but the feel of his fingers and lips on her skin.

It still took him longer than it would when they were alone, but by the time he thrust a finger into her, she was beyond ready, and she cried out as the orgasm consumed her.

Memories of that night always resurfaced whenever she needed something erotic to think about. Lucky for her, she rarely had to come up with fantasies in order to reach orgasm. She had enough real material to work with by now that all she needed to do was slide back into a memory to get off.

What she didn't have in her repertoire, however, was an amazing flogging scene. She'd been flogged many times by various Doms over the years, but neither Nile nor Samson were experts. Samson had dabbled, but he always reverted back to his palm, saying he preferred the direct contact, the warmth of her skin.

Rex increased the pressure, angling his strikes up her back and then down again. There was nothing that could compare to this kind of experience. She felt sorry for anyone who never got the opportunity to be on the receiving end of an excellent flogging.

There was a lot of trust involved, but Rex had already endeared her to him. Any lingering doubts she had were completely unnecessary since Nile was only a few yards away. He would never let anything happen to her. With no worries hanging in the fringes of her mind, she could totally let go and absorb each blow as the thick leather strands continued to rain down on her.

After a while, the floggers disappeared and two hands landed on her back. They rubbed up and down her heated skin. Soft, smooth fingers and palms that belonged to Rex. For a moment, she was surprised, but then she acknowledged that he would stop to check on her. There was no way he would let another Dom ensure she was okay. His lips came close to her ear. "How are you doing, Charlotte?"

She'd been right earlier that morning when she considered the possibility that Rex had a far different persona when he was inside Zodiac than when he was out in the real world. Outside the club, he was more nervous and less confident. As a Dom, he was on his game, never missing a beat. He owned this personality.

"Amazing, Sir. Thank you." Her voice was quiet, but loud enough to let him know she was not completely lost to subspace. She was well-educated when it came to submission. It was important to keep the lines of communication open and ensure whoever dominated her knew where her headspace was.

"Good."

His hands disappeared and another set landed on her bottom, molding to her heated skin. Nile.

She smiled as he kissed her shoulder. "So gorgeous."

"Thank you, Sir."

"Can you take more?"

"Yes, Sir." She sucked in a breath, eager for more, glad to find out they didn't intend to stop just yet.

Nile eased a hand between her legs, pushed her thong aside, and dragged two fingers through her folds. "Mmm. Love when you get wet like this."

She moaned, arching her torso forward. She knew she was soaked. She had been all day. Even the orgasm he'd given her earlier hadn't lessened her desire for more. Of course, it didn't help that he'd only granted her that one completion, settling her on spread knees next, and then tying her hands behind her back before she sucked him off.

While she'd nuzzled his cock for a while afterward, he'd stroked her breasts until she was totally aroused again. And then he'd stopped, leaving her on the edge.

Now... God, she loved the way he reverently touched her pussy, stroking the folds back and forth while avoiding her clit. "Hold on to that feeling. I don't want you to come yet."

"Yes, Sir." Her words were breathy.

When he released her to step back, she heard him sucking her juices off his fingers.

Rex was back in her space a moment later, his hand on her lower back, his body angled toward her at the side. He lifted her chin. "Look at me, Charlotte."

She blinked to focus on his eyes, pleased that he was taking her pulse again.

"You ready to continue?"

"Yes, Sir."

"Safeword?"

"Red, Sir."

He held her gaze for several seconds before releasing her to step behind her again. When the flogging resumed, building in intensity again, she let her body relax and absorb the delicious blows.

Time stood still while the scene went on. More people

gathered, watching and softly admiring. Charlotte grew more aroused by the minute. She knew Nile would recognize the signs when she started to squirm and lean away from the flogger. It wasn't that she didn't want Rex to continue, but this was her way of avoiding an orgasm she didn't have permission to reach. Nile would know.

Sure enough, the flogging slowed to a stop, and Rex was at her back again. His hands once again smoothed over her skin, this time from her shoulders down to her thighs and back up, including cupping her warm bottom briefly. "Your skin is a gorgeous shade of pink."

"Mmm." She rocked into his touch, willing either man to let her come, knowing she absolutely could not ask for the release. Samson would have a field day with that information when she got home.

Rule number two: Either Samson or Nile could grant her an orgasm at their whim. She was not permitted to ask, beg, or in any way insinuate they should let her come.

Rule number two was followed closely by rule number three: She was not permitted to bring herself to orgasm without permission either. If they were not home or she was out of town, she would wait for them to instruct her. Always.

With this in mind, she bit her lip, forcing herself to let Rex and Nile decide what happened next.

Nile stepped up to her side and cupped her breast. He caressed the globe gently, stroking his thumb over her distended nipple. His lips landed on her forehead. A moment later, she sensed Rex taking a step back. He kept one hand on her lower back, but she no longer detected the rest of his warmth.

And then her world shifted.

One moment she was searching her mind for what was going to happen, and the next Rex's flogger struck between her legs, landing on her pussy.

She almost came at the contact. Her breath hitched, and she held it, every ounce of her concentration on the slight, delicious sting. Her clit pulsed, engorged and begging. Her labia were also pulsing.

A second strike landed as Nile flattened his palm on her belly to keep her from rocking forward out of reach. "You are so sexy, baby. How close are you?"

"Nine, Sir," she breathed out. Too close.

"Good. You have permission to come. Let it go."

The leather strips landed once again on her pussy, and then one final time. Two in a row was more than she could endure, and she tipped her head back and cried out as the orgasm consumed her.

The pulsing was delicious. The fact that no one was touching her was frustrating. She needed contact. Anything. Fingers. Inanimate object. Someone's cock. Anything to ease the building pressure. The one orgasm was not enough. It was just a tremor before the earthquake.

As the pulses subsided, Nile slid his hand lower, cupped her pussy from the front, and eased two fingers into her.

She rose onto her tiptoes, gasping at how damn good it felt.

He held her like that, applying the pressure she craved but not moving.

She had to fight to avoid squirming against him, begging nonverbally. It wasn't an offense Nile would punish her for, but he would point it out later.

His lips landed on her ear. "That's my girl. Take what's offered. Not more."

She whimpered.

He kissed behind her ear. "Later, baby. Ease out of it. You aren't permitted to come again right now."

She nodded slightly, biting her lip, forcing her body to simmer down.

Finally, Nile removed his fingers, leaving her panting with need and fidgeting.

Both men released her, one on each side, each lowering her arms and rubbing them to get the blood flowing.

When her ankles were released next, she stepped her feet closer together. A blanket came around her shoulders, and then Nile guided her away from the cross.

He led her to the adjoining room where she'd sat with Rex the night before and chose a sofa with enough space on the other side of her for another person.

She accepted a bottle of water, downed half of it, and closed her eyes, not fully relaxing until she felt the weight of the sofa dip again at her other side, a hand that belonged to Rex coming to her thigh.

She swallowed over an inconvenient revelation.

She liked what had just happened between the three of them.

A lot.

Too much.

What sort of greedy sub needed the attention of yet a third Dom?

CHAPTER 9

Nile left Charlotte sound asleep the next morning and headed down to the hotel gym to get a workout in before she woke up. He left her a note, but he also knew her well enough to assume she would not even move a muscle before he returned.

Charlotte was not a morning person. In addition, she was wiped out from last night. It had been really late when he brought her back to the hotel. The moment they'd stepped inside, he'd told her to strip and began removing his own clothing. He'd been hard for hours, but hadn't wanted to fuck her at the club.

Nile wasn't too shy to take her occasionally in public, but something about the evening had made him hold back. The scene with Rex had been phenomenal. The two of them had immediately established a rapport and then fell into sync.

Charlotte had blown his mind when she'd come from the flogger between her legs. So fucking sexy. Incredible.

He'd needed her, and he'd waited until they got back to the hotel to take her hard and fast.

As he entered the gym, he was glad to find it empty. He put

on his headphones, started the treadmill, and then called Samson.

"Hey. I wondered when you might call. Didn't want to wake you. It's early. How late did you stay at Zodiac?"

"Late. Really late, but I couldn't sleep any longer. Charlotte is still zonked out of course."

"Let me guess. You're on the treadmill."

"Yep. I'll get a few miles in and then go wake her up. She has a meeting this afternoon with the realtor and then we'll head to the airport."

"So, how'd it go last night?"

"It was indescribable. I've seriously never seen Charlotte so worked up."

"Did this guy, Rex, flog her again?"

"Yes. We worked together. He flogged. I soothed. I had him bring her to orgasm with the swat of that leather between her legs."

"No shit?"

"Yep. She might have enjoyed it a bit much."

"I was afraid of that."

Nile glanced around to make sure he was still alone. "You would have been impressed. Who knew there might be yet another Dom hanging around who could get under Charlotte's skin and give her something neither you nor I provide?"

"Impressive. Are you concerned?"

"Not really." He sighed. "Okay, maybe a little. She knew the guy in high school. Not well, and it's been a long time, but it still establishes history. For some people that can be comforting."

"Yeah." Samson inhaled long and slow. "Well, all you can do is head back here tonight. We'll confront her soon and take her pulse. If she wants to explore something outside of our arrangement, we can't stop her."

"Well, we can. But we both know we would never do that. It would only push her away."

"Exactly."

"See you tonight."

"Yep. Later."

Nile tapped the screen to disconnect the call and then picked up the pace. He needed to run hard to put his worries aside for a while.

~

Nile had to gently nudge Charlotte to wake her up when they pulled into the underground parking garage of their apartment. She had been quiet most of the day. Pensive.

She leaned against his side as they rode to the top floor in the elevator, slowly coming more awake. Eventually, she smiled at him. He would have hugged her, but he was holding their bags in each of his hands.

Samson met them at the door, pulled a sleepy Charlotte into his side with one arm, and set his other hand on Nile's shoulder. He met Nile's gaze before addressing Charlotte. "Successful trip? How'd it go today with the realtor?"

"It went well, I think. The property is in a nice location. Busy strip mall. It would work for me, but the price is a bit steep. It needs some work. The previous owner left it kind of trashed, and the layout isn't quite right for a boutique. We'll see. Still negotiating."

"Well, if it's meant to be, it will work out." Samson helped her out of her coat and then hung it on a hook by the door while Charlotte removed the rest of her clothes. Even though there was an odd vibe in the air, she didn't break from the routine.

As soon as she was naked, Samson helped her into a silk robe and took her hand. "It's late, sweetheart. Let's get you to

73

bed." He led her down the hallway to the master bedroom and released her, pointing toward the attached bath.

She entered and shut the door. They had always granted her privacy in the bathroom.

Samson lifted a brow.

Nile shrugged as he kicked off his shoes. What could he say? He didn't know more than what he'd divulged that morning. He too was tired. He needed sleep. They all did. Tomorrow was Monday. They all had to work. Maybe returning to the daily grind would ease the tension.

They didn't always sleep in the same bed. They each had their own room and their own space. But it seemed important to surround her with their strength tonight of all nights. So, Nile removed all but his briefs and then padded down the hallway to the hall bath to brush his teeth.

Ten minutes later, they were under the covers, Nile on one side of Charlotte, Samson on the other. Samson draped an arm over her belly and kissed her temple. Nile nestled his arm against Samson's, clasping the other man's bicep while he waited for Charlotte to settle. It took a while for her to slide into a deep sleep, but Nile didn't relax until she did so. Finally, he blew out a breath and closed his eyes.

They'd opened a Pandora's box. There was no going back. Only forward.

Although the three of them had enjoyed this living arrangement for three years, it wasn't legally binding by any stretch. No one was married among them. They'd also carefully dodged the L-word.

There had been times when Nile had considered telling Charlotte how he felt, but by unspoken agreement, he held his tongue. There were three of them. It would be wrong for one person to declare something deeper to another, leaving the third party blindsided.

In the back of his mind, Nile had always known there

might come a day when one of them needed or wanted something different. Any one of them could have met someone and moved on.

They'd gotten complacent. Or at least he had. This situation worked. It worked for all of them. Until it didn't. Had that day come?

Maybe he was making more out of this than necessary. Maybe Charlotte had enjoyed a couple scenes with a different sort of Dom and could move on now.

He didn't believe that in his heart, though. And ignoring the shift under their feet would not be wise. They needed to discuss it and figure it out. Together.

CHAPTER 10

Charlotte was usually the last to leave the house most mornings. After all, her boutiques opened at ten, and she had capable employees at every location. Nile usually needed to meet with his own employees earlier than that, and Samson often headed for his gym before dawn.

Both men were hanging back this morning. She knew there were things that needed to be said. But not before work. The discussion would take longer than a few minutes and involve emotions she wasn't ready to face.

Nile had showered with her and helped her dress. Samson had made her a power smoothie which he brought into the bathroom. They hadn't remained in silence, but their conversation revolved around each of their plans for the day.

By the time she arrived at her first boutique, she was stressed.

In addition to tiptoeing around both men all morning, it was notable that they hadn't had sex. That was rare. Not unheard of, but rare. Ordinarily she would have found herself well-sated by at least Samson, whom she hadn't seen for several days.

She also hadn't stopped thinking about Rex. He kept creeping into her mind. As soon as she checked in with her employees and settled in the back office to look over the books, she took out her phone and sent a brief text to Rex.

Just wanted to say how much I enjoyed my weekend. Thank you so much for everything.

She chewed on her bottom lip while she stared at the words after she sent them. Suddenly they sounded absurd. And then she nearly jumped out of her skin when the phone vibrated in her hand, indicating there was an incoming call from Rex. She tapped the screen to answer it. It wasn't as if she could ignore it since she was clearly holding the phone. "Hey," she said, trying to sound casual.

"Hey, yourself. You make it home okay?"

"Yep. No problems. Slept hard, and I'm already at work."

"You slept well?"

She swallowed and then closed her eyes and rubbed her forehead. "Well... no."

He chuckled nervously. "Do you lie to Samson and Nile like that?"

"No. Never." This was fucking awkward.

"I didn't think so. What we did was rather intense. I was worried about you."

She took a few shallow breaths. "What about you? I wasn't the only one there."

"Yeah," he breathed out softly. "You're right about that. I don't usually get mindfucked by a scene, but it would be wrong of me to pretend I wasn't affected."

"Yeah," she repeated back to him in a similar tone. "I think you gave me something different. Something I'm not used to. And it made me take notice." She couldn't believe she was having this conversation. She shouldn't even be discussing this with Rex before she spoke to her Doms.

"Will you be coming back to Denver again soon?"

"Not sure yet. Still negotiating that property. But probably. If that one falls through, I'll still be looking."

"Right. Well, stay in touch. Let me know if you're in town and you want to scene again or whatever."

The word *whatever* hung in the air like a suggestion she wasn't willing to ponder. As if Rex would be willing to scene with her or do anything else with her.

"I will." She bit her lip, pondering the implications. Why did her heart rate pick up at the mention of submitting to him again? This was bad. She never thought twice about Doms she submitted to. They were just scenes. Nothing more.

"Tell Nile I said hi. Hopefully next time I'll meet Samson."

"Yeah, maybe." She forced a smile into her voice.

"Take care, Charlotte."

"You too." She ended the call and slumped back in her chair.

Part of her felt like she'd just cheated on two men. They didn't have the sort of arrangement that was intended to be permanent or binding, but they were open and discussed every single detail of their lives.

This morning's conversation with Rex needed to be divulged, and soon. Tonight. Hell, they needed to have a huge discussion later. Hopefully they would both be available for dinner.

Charlotte dropped her purse on the table next to the front door as soon as she entered the penthouse and removed her clothes, folding them and setting them on the shelf where she always did. Noises came from deeper in the house while she slid into the hot pink silk robe she found hanging from a hook.

As she finished, Samson padded toward her. "How was your day?"

"Not bad, Sir. Yours?"

"Pretty good as well. Nile is cooking."

She inhaled deeply and smiled. It smelled wonderful. "Italian, Sir?"

"Yep. He's in his usual mode, making fresh pasta and sauce. If anyone ever finds out how damn lucky we are, they will probably stab us both in our sleep and claim our spots."

"God, I hope not, Sir." She followed him toward the kitchen and let him lift her onto a stool at the island.

Nile wiped his hands on a towel and came around to kiss her briefly on the lips. "Ooh, I like that robe," he stated, leaning back and then glancing at Samson. "We should invest in more sexy lingerie. The mystery of something new always makes my mouth water." He winked and then returned to the stove.

"Well, Christmas is in a few weeks. You just never know what I might have purchased while you two were gone this weekend." His devious smile made her heart flutter.

Steam was wafting from several pots and pans, and the rich smell of red sauce filled the room.

She had texted both of them earlier in the day to see if they would be home for dinner, and they had both responded yes. She hadn't expected this kind of reception, but she would never complain when Nile got home early enough to cook. Neither would Samson. There was a reason Nile's catering business was such a success.

Samson handed her a glass of red wine, and she took a sip, moaning around the flavor. He leaned an elbow on the counter next to her and met her gaze. "I know we need to talk about this past weekend, but let's eat first and then get frank. Okay?"

"Yes, Sir." She smiled, trying not to feel nervous. There was no reason to be. This was Samson and Nile she was talking to. Not strangers. These were her Doms. The men who made her heart race and her life beyond amazing. She needed to get over whatever weird thing had ahold of her and get back to her regularly scheduled life.

Samson scurried around helping Nile get dinner on the table while Charlotte sat like the princess they treated her as and watched them. There were nights when she did the cooking. There were more nights when none of them cooked because it was rare that they were all home early enough.

They chatted about work over the delicious meal of pasta, sauce, salad, and French bread. After the men cleared the dishes away, they moved to the spacious living room and each took a spot on the sectional, not touching, facing each other.

Charlotte curled her feet under her and met their gazes. The time for submitting was on hold in an unspoken agreement. She needed to start this conversation. "I spoke to Rex this morning. I texted him to thank him for the weekend, and he called."

Both men nodded. "How did that go?" Samson asked. "It sounds like he rocked your world a bit. I think we need to talk about it."

"Yeah," she breathed, unsure what to say next. She cleared her throat. "I'm flustered, to be honest. I've never been quite so shaken by anyone in the three years we've been living together."

"We can see that, baby," Nile agreed. "And you need to know that no one is angry or even frustrated with you. This arrangement is meant to be one where we can speak freely and discuss anything."

"He's right, sweetheart. I don't want you to feel like we're ganging up on you either. We just want the lines of communication open."

"I know. And I appreciate it. I just don't know exactly what to say. It's not complicated really. Rex dominated me, and I liked it." It really wasn't more than that, right?

"Except it wasn't quite that simple, was it?" Nile added. "I was there the second night. I saw your reaction. It wasn't just a scene you walked away from and shook off. He got under your skin."

"Yeah..."

Samson leaned forward, putting his elbows on his knees. "And that's okay. It happens. You can't control your reaction to people."

She leaned her head back and addressed the ceiling. "Can't I, though? I mean what woman could possibly be in a relationship with two of the best Doms on earth and glance twice at any other human?"

Nile chuckled. "Charlotte, you're human. Everyone glances at other humans."

She lifted her face and met his gaze. "You know it was more than that."

"I do. I get it."

Samson spoke again. "I think you need to take some time to think about what happened and how you felt. We aren't judging you for enjoying another Dom's method of dominance. It's natural. What happens next is what we need to figure out, but we don't have to solve anything today or even this week. All we ask is that you keep talking to us."

She held Samson's gaze. "I don't see either of you dominating another person and getting all twisted up in it." She chewed on her bottom lip, trying not to cry. She felt awful. This was so out of control. How on earth could she have feelings for yet another man? What the fuck was wrong with her?

And why were the two of them being so accommodating? They should be angry or at least nervous. Instead, they were laid back and open-minded. Part of her felt like they were using this bonkers situation to get her to leave them. But that made no sense either. Why cook her dinner, pamper her, and treat her like they adored her if their goal was to break up with her?

Samson shrugged. "We aren't you. We knew you enjoyed a lot of dominance and spending a lot of time submitting when we met you. You knew before I stepped into the picture that you wanted more than you got from Nile. That has never been a question."

"And I felt like shit about it," she pointed out, shifting her gaze to Nile.

He took a deep breath. "Baby, I was never mad. I knew it. I was never going to be the sort of Dom who could strike your skin. It's not in me. I was beyond ecstatic when we met Samson and easily turned this into a threesome. Both Samson and I get exactly what we want and need from our arrangement, and you get two Doms who fulfill two different needs."

"How many damn needs am I allowed to have?" she asked, her voice rising. She ran a hand through her hair and groaned. "The majority of people aren't so greedy that they can't handle life with just one partner."

Nile lifted both shoulders. "Who cares how everyone else lives? They aren't us. I've never been convinced any of them were happy either. Not the people who insist on being completely vanilla at least. After watching nearly every acquaintance I have go in and out of relationships, often fighting and breaking up, I've come to realize no one really has the secret to happiness, but our situation sure comes closer than most."

"He's right," Samson added. "Like I said, the important thing is that we keep talking about it. We'll figure this out. I don't want you worrying about saying or doing the wrong things. You won't be happy if you shove your feelings down deep and try to conform to some norm that we don't believe in anyway. So what if you feel a connection to another Dom? There's nothing wrong with enjoying another type of submission. Maybe he could come visit."

She gasped. "That's getting ahead of things a bit." *Right?*

Samson shrugged. "I'm just saying, take a breath, let yourself feel, and let's see what happens." He crawled her direction. When he reached her side, he cupped her face and held her gaze. "It's all going to work out just fine."

Nile stood and came to her other side, his hand landing on her shoulder. "He's right. Do what you need to do. Talk to Rex if you feel like it. Invite him to visit if you want. We'll support you no matter what."

A tear leaked. She really loved these two. They had never said it out loud, but she loved them all the same. Even through the conflicting emotions, she still loved them both fiercely.

Maybe she just needed to remind herself how amazing her life was. It was the best life of anyone she knew. Her greed was unnecessary. She would shake it off and pull herself together. Rocking this boat was stupidity.

She reached for both of them, and then smiled as they leaned in, each kissing her neck as their hands roamed up her body.

Emotions welled up inside her, but something was wrong. Just slightly tilted. As her eyes slid closed, she realized that while the L word was on the tip of her tongue, not just tonight, but often, neither of them had ever used the word either. How serious did they feel about her?

Anytime they came together to touch base and take one another's pulses, Nile and Samson always insisted it would all "work out just fine." That was so vague. She'd begun to wonder if this entire arrangement was far more laissez-faire for them than it was for her.

CHAPTER 11

It had been a week since Rex had his hands on Charlotte's skin. A very long week. He also hadn't communicated with her since Monday morning. He couldn't decide whose court the ball was in. On the one hand, she'd texted him first. On the other hand, he'd called her.

He'd be lying to himself if he didn't admit he'd loved hearing her voice. He'd loved even more touching her skin last weekend. But the most intense memory he had was her coming from the simple stroke of his flogger against her pussy.

He closed his eyes and inhaled deeply as he recalled every detail. The way she moaned softly as her body shook. The way her face softened, the corners of her lips tipping up as the pulses subsided. The way her mouth fell open when she gasped. The way her breasts shook and her nipples stood out stiff and hard.

And then there was the connection she had with Nile. Comfortable. Easy. Loving. Rex could tell by the look in her eyes that she was deeply committed to Nile. Nile adored her too. He rarely took his gaze off her, his mouth turned up in a permanent smile when she was nearby.

Rex wondered if she had that same connection with Samson, and if so, why was she giving Rex the time of day?

He reminded himself that the world was filled with all kinds of submissives. Maybe Charlotte was the kind of person who needed more, who liked to explore. Someone who enjoyed an open sexual relationship.

Although Rex was ridiculously attracted to her, he wasn't at all convinced he could or should do anything about it. Even if Nile and Samson were both open to letting her play with Rex, did Rex want to be that outsider who scened with another Dom's sub? Or two Doms in this case?

Granted, he scened with other Doms' subs often, but not like this. Not someone he decidedly wished he could sleep with. Not someone he wanted to hold in the night and wake up to in the morning. That was crossing the line.

He tried to visualize a world where he shared a submissive with other Doms. What did they do? Take turns sleeping with her at night? Or did they all sleep in the same bed? Did Nile and Samson also have a sexual relationship?

God. This could not be happening. Rex didn't have answers. He hadn't considered any of these options before. He'd never found himself in this kind of situation. And hell, was he really in any kind of "situation" at all right now? So, he'd spent a weekend with Charlotte, including one of her Doms in the second half. It probably meant nothing to her. He might never hear from her again.

But there was a connection between them. He knew it. And he needed to know more. He couldn't stop thinking about the entire event and the implications. How open Nile had been. How open they both insinuated Samson was also. Rex would not be able to let this sleeping dog lie.

Something about the entire arrangement tugged at him.

Not just Charlotte. The whole package. He couldn't put his finger on it.

Rex forced himself to turn on his stool and glance around at Club Zodiac in full swing. It was late. The club was packed. And he was still sitting at the bar nursing a soda. Same as last night.

"Let me guess..." The voice coming from Rex's left made him turn that direction to find Colin taking the seat next to him. "A certain strawberry-blond beauty tore you to shreds and tossed the pieces to the wind." He smiled, but it was more of an understanding look of commiseration.

Rex smirked and rubbed a hand down his face. "I have no idea how or why I let someone get under my skin. It's never happened before. I scene with dozens of people. It's something I'm good at. I don't get involved with them. I don't fall for them."

Colin shrugged. "Eventually we all fall for someone. I was blindsided when I first started seeing Rayne. She had me in knots all the time. Here I was working night and day to get this club open while tripping over myself to catch the eye of a woman who I wasn't sure could click with me in the lifestyle." Colin twisted to look Rex in the eye. "Did you know Rayne used to date Rowen?"

Rex shook his head. He didn't think he'd heard this story before. He'd met Rowen several times. He was one of the owners of the Miami Club Zodiac. He was also married to a woman named Faith. They had visited Denver together.

"Yep. The two of them didn't meet at Zodiac. She wasn't in the lifestyle at all at the time. The two of them tried hard but were never really right for each other. When they finally broke up, she realized it wasn't the kink that was her problem. Turned out, she wasn't with the right Dom." Colin smiled and straightened to sit taller in an exaggerated caveman move. He came just shy of pounding his chest.

Rex chuckled. "Uh-huh. Thank God the right man finally showed her what it's all about."

Colin laughed. "Exactly. Though I'll deny it if you breathe a word of that to Rayne."

Rex shook his head. What the hell did this have to do with him?

"My point is that sometimes you meet someone whose kink matches yours. It's a gift. Granted, I realize you only did two scenes with Charlotte, but anyone watching could see the chemistry between you. You're an expert flogger, and she craved what you could give her with every inch of her body. The connection was palpable."

Rex lifted a brow. "Even if you're right, what good is that doing me since she lives in Seattle with not one but two Doms?"

Colin shrugged. "I didn't say life was easy. I'm just stating the obvious. Nor am I suggesting you rush in and try to break up her current relationship. I don't know her other Dom, Samson, but I do know Nile, and he's a great guy. One of the good ones. It was clear to me that he worships Charlotte. They have an undeniable rapport. I'm just pointing out that so did the two of you. In fact, you got along splendidly with Nile too. Maybe it was the triad that intrigued you. You haven't really entered into one of those before." He leaned back, setting his elbows on the counter.

Rex turned to face the room, pondering Colin's words. Honestly, Rex had a lot to think about. For one thing, he hadn't really expected to find someone he clicked with at any point. He was by far the nerdiest guy he knew. Sure, maybe he'd grown up some and matured a bit since high school, but inside, he still fit the term brainiac.

He knew he was a math genius. Numbers came naturally to him. He was wired for it. For some odd reason, he was never tormented in school. Other students respected him instead of making fun of him. He figured he had his mother to thank for some of that. She made sure he was dressed the same as other kids, wore a stylish haircut for the times and owned appropriate toys. She couldn't completely cover up his oddity, but she did make it better.

At twenty-eight, he was a grown adult who fit in with society considerably better than he had as a child. Nevertheless, his brain still worked differently from others. He managed to assume a far more confident personality the moment he stepped into the club, but out in the real world, he was still awkward. Women he dated often found him too intimidating.

Not Charlotte. She hadn't flinched. Granted, their interaction hadn't extended much past negotiating and then performing a scene. He couldn't really know how she might feel about him if they went to dinner and a movie.

What the hell was he even thinking? He was never going on a date with Charlotte. *She has two Doms.* Apparently, Colin didn't think he should shoot down the idea of reaching out to her even though she was in a committed relationship, but that was way outside of Rex's comfort zone.

"You didn't scene with anyone last night. You got anything lined up for tonight?" Colin asked.

"Nope."

Colin chuckled as he shoved from his seat. "Don't write it off. I'm telling you. You never know."

He did know, though. He knew the first woman he'd really clicked with in any fashion, both inside and outside the club, wasn't available to him. He knew she lived in Seattle. He knew he was wasting his time thinking about her so obsessively.

∾

His resolve to move on lasted until Wednesday. When he rationalized he could text her. She'd texted him last week. He could text her this time. Bearing in mind there was a possibility two other people might read her texts.

How did it go with the property you were looking at in Denver? I've been wondering.

He intentionally walked away from his phone after sending that text, forcing himself to make a sandwich for lunch. It was almost noon. He took his time, arranging the turkey and cheese just right on the bread. Adding lettuce and slices of tomato and then mayonnaise. He grabbed a small bag of chips and a bottle of water.

Instead of sitting in silence, he told Alexa to play Christmas music. That would distract him. After eating, while humming along to the latest pop version of "Santa Baby," he wandered over to his small tree and straightened several ornaments, obsessing over their distance from one another like the dorky mathematician he was.

Finally, he returned to his desk and glared at the phone that lay face down, tempting him. Thank God he was working from home this week. He'd spent so much time staring at that phone and pacing with it in the last week, an office full of people would have thought he'd lost his marbles.

He finally yanked up the phone.

The breath whooshed from his lungs when he saw a reply.

Ugh. It fell through. I couldn't rationalize the asking price since it needed so much renovation, and the owner wasn't willing to budge. Thank you for asking. My realtor has already lined up another property, however, which is hard to believe with just two weeks left until Christmas. I'm going to fly in tomorrow in fact to look at it. I keep intending to call or text you to let you know, but I've been so busy.

Rex's heart raced and he couldn't stop the rapid rise and fall of his chest as he read and reread her message. She was coming to Denver again. Tomorrow. That made him feel like jumping up and down with elation. However, she also hadn't told him and perhaps wouldn't have at all if he hadn't reached out.

He had no idea how to read into this information. Nor could he think how to respond. He was still holding the phone and staring at it when it rang in his hand. He smiled as he saw her name. Now they were even, he thought as he answered it. "Hey." He tried hard to sound nonchalant. No way could she see him smoothing his shirt or making sure it was tucked in.

"Hey, yourself. I'm so sorry. When I read that message, I realized I sounded like I never meant to call."

"It's okay," he responded, forcing himself to sound light. Inside, he was twisted in knots like a teenager speaking to the head cheerleader.

She sighed. "I promise I wouldn't have shown up without saying a word. In fact, Samson is coming with me, and we'll be at Zodiac Friday night. Will you be there? I'd love for you to meet him. Maybe we could do a scene together?"

He swallowed past the lump in his throat. So many emotions. He couldn't begin to wrap his mind around how Charlotte managed to squeeze his heart so tightly. It wasn't logical. They'd done two scenes together and had coffee. No one should be this intrigued by a woman they barely knew.

But he was. Or at least the idea of her. Maybe this would be perfect. Surely he'd blown everything about her out of proportion in his mind. If he did another scene with her, he could rejoin reality and shake free of her. After all, she was bringing her other Dom with her.

He remembered her telling him Samson was the disciplinarian of the group. He was a spanker.

Rex suddenly realized it was his turn to speak. "That sounds good. If Samson has anything special in mind he'd like to do Friday, have him call me. I'll make the arrangements."

"Oh. That's a good idea." The pitch of her voice was higher. "I love secrets and surprises. I'll have him call you. You two can make arrangements. If you don't mind, I mean. I don't want to intrude on any plans you already have."

"Nope. No particular plans. I'll block out a slot. Give Samson my number."

"Awesome. I'm excited already." He could hear the growing lift in her voice. It made him smile to know she was so pleased.

"Well, I better get back to work." He didn't want her to realize how damn eager he was, nor how worried he was at the same time. This entire thing could go one of two ways. He might see her with Samson and know he didn't stand a chance. Or, he might figure out that every daydream he'd had since he'd last seen her had been true. That he was indeed into her in a way he had no business feeling. In which case, he would be doomed to feel worse next week than he had after she left the first time.

There were no other options here. He had to know one way or the other. If not, he would slowly lose his mind.

"Right. I'm supposed to be in a meeting in a few minutes too. Hope the rest of your day is smooth. Looking forward to Friday."

"Me too. See you then." He ended the call and set the phone on his desk. Holy shit. When he'd sent the text, he'd never dreamed fifteen minutes later he would find himself even more into her with a scene to plan for two days from now.

CHAPTER 12

Samson didn't call until Friday afternoon. By then, Rex had been pacing his apartment for the better part of two days. He'd developed a bit of a complex too, thinking when Charlotte had told Samson to call Rex, he'd laughed at her and declined. That was possible. Though Rex had a hard time picturing her with anyone who would make light of any request she made.

Finally, the phone rang with an unknown number with a Seattle area code.

Rex took a deep breath and answered. "Hello?"

"Hi. Is this Rex Kyle?"

"It is."

"This is Samson Sutherland. I'm sorry it took me so long to get ahold of you. Charlotte asked me to call Wednesday, but I haven't had a chance until just now."

"No problem. Did you make it to Denver yesterday?"

"Yes. We're actually out looking at a few properties right now. I stepped outside to call you while Charlotte talks to the realtor."

Outside? It was damn cold outside. Granted, Charlotte had

said Samson owned a gym. At the moment, Rex was picturing a gigantic buff man in a tight T-shirt, undaunted by the temperature. He shook the absurd thought from his mind. "Will you be able to break away for some time at Zodiac tonight? Charlotte mentioned me securing a time slot and an apparatus."

"Yes. That's still the plan. Is that okay? I know it's late notice."

"It's perfectly fine. I'll call Colin and make sure he gets us on the schedule when we hang up."

"Perfect. Now, what do you have in mind? I know Charlotte is a little taken with you. She's been nearly bouncing off the walls at the thought of doing another scene with you." His voice was light. Friendly. But holy fuck this was awkward.

Taken? Bouncing? Jesus. "I assumed you and I would work together. Tell me which apparatus you usually prefer, if any. I could get a private room too if you'd like."

"Mmm. How do you feel about setting up a situation where she's intentionally meant to be defiant, therefore requiring punishment? We haven't done that in a while. Nile and I used to plot devious scenes like that, but we haven't taken the time lately."

Rex lifted both brows. Until last weekend, he'd rarely shared a scene with another Dom. He'd never set anything up ahead of time that included role play in which the submissive might behave naughty intentionally in order to get punished. Hell, he wasn't really a disciplinarian at all. It was outside of his comfort zone. But this could work. He was certainly willing to try. "Sounds intriguing. I assume you're going to be the one to punish her after I set her up for failure."

"Yep. Disciplining her is my specialty. What other items are you proficient in besides floggers?"

"Oh, I can strike with just about anything, though I'm

hesitant with anything that could draw blood, especially with someone with skin as fair as Charlotte. How about a silicone paddle?"

"Perfect. I like it." He sounded excited. "I'll fill her in on the stakes. I never enter any scene without making sure she's clear on the plan. Not the details, but our expectations and goals."

"Perfect. I'll block out some time for us."

"Sounds good. I better get back inside. We'll see you at about eleven."

"See you then." Rex was shaking as he ended the call. He was both excited and nervous. He could visualize the scene he had in mind clearly. This was a new challenge for him. He knew what he wanted to do. He'd simply never acted out something so specific.

Before he did anything else, he popped an email to Colin, requesting a private room. The last thing he wanted was an audience for his first foray into this type of role play. If it didn't go exactly as planned, he would prefer only the three of them be privy to the experience.

CHAPTER 13

Charlotte was on pins and needles as she changed into the outfit Nile had selected for her and packed in a black bag so she couldn't easily see it until just now. The fact that Nile had chosen her clothes for tonight wasn't odd at all. The fact that he'd hidden his selection had made her squirm. She knew it was his way of peripherally participating. Even though he wouldn't be present, at least he would have contributed in some fashion.

She took a deep breath and opened the bag. And then she smiled. The naughty school girl outfit. Apropos considering he hadn't known what specific type of scene they would plan before she'd left the house yesterday.

Hell, she barely understood the scene as it was now. She knew exactly what was necessary and not a single bit more.

Rex would start the scene with some sort of play that would make it difficult for her to obey his orders. Samson would step in later and punish her for her misbehavior. She'd been wet since the moment Samson filled her in two hours ago.

Of course, she'd been naked at the time. He hadn't

permitted her to dress in warm clothes until it was time to leave the hotel. Nile and Samson had started wearing T-shirts and shorts in the penthouse in order to keep the temperature warm enough for her in her constant state of near nudity. Tonight, Samson had also been the one to carry the bag with her change of clothes in it.

The drive to the club had made her giddy with excitement. She wasn't sure if it was anticipation or the way the city was so festively lit up with strings of Christmas lights that hung in nearly every store front. It was impossible not to get excited during the holidays.

She loved having formed a family unit in Seattle. It gave her people to be with during the holidays. Denver wasn't that far away, but after her father had passed, her mother had moved to Florida to join lifelong friends of hers, and she seemed perfectly fine spending Christmas with them.

It was possible that because Charlotte had hinted at her relationship status, her mother had been uncomfortable with it and didn't want to face it. So, taking the plunge with two men had alienated her a bit with her mom, which was both good and bad. They had a silent agreement. Charlotte never mentioned Nile and Samson, while her mother never mentioned a word about Charlotte's lifestyle choice.

It wasn't as if Nile and Samson were chomping at the bit to spend Christmas with their families either. They each had their own issues.

She returned her focus to getting dressed. Leaving her black lace thong on, she grabbed the skirt first and zipped up the side. It was a red and black plaid and it didn't quite cover her butt cheeks, which made goose bumps rise on her ass and thighs.

She didn't have a bra. Samson hadn't permitted her to wear one under her warmer clothes, nor had he packed one in the mystery bag. Not shocking. She put the white blouse on next. The material was thin enough that it left nothing to the imagination, and it had no buttons. Instead, it tied off between her breasts.

After securing the knot, she stared in a full-length mirror and took in the several inches of skin between the skirt and the blouse. Next, she sat on a bench to put on the knee-high white socks and then the red Converse. Unsure what they might expect her to do with her hair, she decided to divide it in half and put it up in two high ponytails. A true school girl.

By the time she was ready to leave the room, she was fully feeling the role.

She was also horny.

It didn't take long to find her men at the bar, and she approached them with her hands clasped at her lower back, head bowed. Her emotions were all over the place. She was excited to see Rex again, but her stomach was twisted in knots at the prospect of doing a scene with Samson and Rex.

It wasn't the sort of nervousness that came from worry. All three of them knew the odd stakes here. It had more to do with anticipation mixed with arousal. After the way things went with Rex and Nile a few weeks ago, she had no doubt tonight would be equally titillating. Albeit different.

Samson reached out a hand and tucked her into his side, his other hand going to her hair to tug on one of the ponytails. "I like this. Good job, sweetheart."

She smiled. Her heart warmed any time he complimented her. "Thank you, Sir."

"I understand Nile chose this outfit for you before you left Seattle," Rex said.

Charlotte's body heated further at the sound of Rex's voice. The memory of it had faded. Now that he was speaking to her again in person, she melted. She was in so much trouble if just the sound of his voice could make her take notice. "Yes, Sir."

"Good choice. I think you'll be the perfect naughty school girl in a few minutes."

She swallowed, a shiver racing down her body. Nothing sounded better than role-playing with two men. Except maybe three men...

"I arranged a private room," Rex continued. "It's ready for us."

Samson slid a hand down Charlotte's thigh and then up under her skirt to squeeze her butt cheek. "Ready, sweetheart?"

"Yes, Sir." *Beyond ready.*

She followed Rex down a hallway lined with rooms on both sides. The doors had glass panels, and some of them were blocked off from the inside with curtains.

As they entered a dimly lit room on the left, Samson stepped into her space from behind and set his hands on her hips. "Your job is to do as you're told. If you can manage that, you won't be punished."

"Yes, Sir." She sucked in a breath, finally realizing the plan. Rex would undoubtedly be the one to start this scene, and he would be making demands she would eventually fail to comply with. He might be the rocket scientist in the room, but it didn't take one to figure out the game plan.

She didn't fully lift her gaze, but she did take in the room. It was entirely burgundy. The paint, the carpet, and the padded leather platform in the middle.

Samson ran his hands up and down her biceps, leaning in to speak close to her ear. "Rex suggested we do this scene in private. Since the three of us have never performed together, we want you to be relaxed and comfortable without worrying about who's watching."

"Thank you, Sir." She didn't have a problem performing in public, but it could be unnerving in a situation where she didn't have all the information. Unlike her arrangement with

Nile and Rex the last time she'd been here, this scene included role play that wouldn't be fully spelled out to her ahead of time.

"Safeword?" Samson asked. He didn't remind her of her ability to bail every time they played any more. She knew. It was ingrained in her. But since they were working with Rex, it was appropriate for him to remind her.

"Red, Sir."

"Good girl. Use it if you get nervous."

She nodded.

He gave her bottom a light swat. "Climb up on the platform. Do as you're told."

She shuffled forward, releasing her hands from behind her back to set them on the leather as she crawled onto the surface. It was cool against her skin. The platform itself was almost like a bed, approximately four feet wide and six feet long. A person could be stretched out on it, attached at the corners. She wondered if Rex intended to restrain her.

"Hands and knees, Charlotte," Rex instructed. "Crawl into the center."

She obeyed his demand, situating herself so that her knees were about a foot wide. With her head tipped down, she could see her breasts swaying free, the blouse barely covering them. The brush of the material against her nipples aroused her further.

She closed her eyes as Rex began to circle the platform. She could sense him at all times. She didn't need to see him to picture him in her mind. Black jeans, navy button-up shirt, black loafers. His skin was almost as pale as hers, but he wasn't the scrawny sort of math geek one would expect. He worked out. His biceps were built. His pecs were solid.

When he stopped at the foot of the platform, he crouched down to pull something out from under it. She opened her eyes to watch him between her legs, but he didn't make eye contact.

Seconds later, he was standing again, holding something black in his hand. Not a flogger. Something else. When he slapped it against his palm, she realized it was a paddle. Rubber perhaps. Somewhat flexible.

She inhaled slowly. Apparently floggers weren't his only specialty. Why hadn't that occurred to her? Of course the man had other implements. Luckily, she knew what it felt like to be swatted with silicone. She'd experienced it before. But the anticipation of having someone new use it on her hovered in the air anyway.

Rex set the flat rubber paddle against the back of her thigh and rubbed it up and down from her knee to her butt. He did this to the other leg next and then stepped closer to lift her skirt over her cheeks and settle it on her back. "You may drop to your elbows, Charlotte. Rest your forehead against the platform."

She did as he instructed, grateful because she felt much more stable on her elbows than her palms. Her nipples danced against the leather in this position, nothing but the thin material of her blouse between them and the cool surface. They stiffened.

"Knees wider."

She parted her thighs at his command, already more aroused than she should have been. She had an unusual comfort level with Rex that shouldn't exist after only two previous scenes with him. He was so...attentive. Invested in this scene. It was titillating in a way she hadn't experienced lately. Although she submitted to Nile and Samson every day of her life, neither of them had gone out of their way to set up something thoughtful and original lately.

Was her attraction to Rex based on the newness? The unexpected? His ability to use an instrument neither of her

Doms yielded? She didn't have the answers, but her mind was open to whatever delicious experience she was about to endure.

Rex tapped her butt cheeks back and forth, gently, giving her the smallest taste for what was about to come.

She was aware of Samson moving around her, but suddenly he surprised her by sitting on the platform near her head. He set a hand on the back of her neck and stroked her tense muscles. A moment later, his hand eased to one of her ponytails, and he drew his palm down the strands before repeating the action.

A relatively hard swat of the paddle took her by surprise, making her rock forward at the same time she curled her toes under and dug them into the leather beneath her shoes.

"Ah, sweetheart. No moving. Your job is to remain still while Rex swats your pretty bottom to a deep pink."

"Yes, Sir." His first swat hadn't hurt badly; it had simply taken her by surprise. She needed to get a hold of herself. They were just getting started and already she was flinching.

Rex gave another swat, this one lighter, and then he paddled her other cheek with a bit more force. She quickly realized there would be no pattern. No rhythm. Not like when he used the floggers on her. This scene would be different.

He lowered the paddle and tapped her thigh next. "I love how quickly your skin pinkens. It's so gorgeous."

"Thank you, Sir."

He rained several more strikes up and down her thighs, switching back and forth, making her sway a bit. "No moving, Charlotte. Remain perfectly still."

She squeezed her eyes closed, concentrating as he struck her butt cheek again, increasing the force. It burned deliciously. Erotically. So damn good. She could easily lose herself in this scene.

Samson continued to run his fingers through her

ponytails, alternating back and forth, dropping them next to her cheek in between. It reminded her constantly of his presence. His part in this scene.

She swayed again. It was too much of a struggle to remain still.

"If you can't keep from moving, you'll be punished," Rex informed her.

She swallowed, unable to respond. Her pussy clenched, wetness soaking her thong. Her breasts were heavy, her nipples dragging against the platform over and over with each swat. The slight jolt was unavoidable.

Rex continued to spank her with the paddle, heating her skin, making her crave contact with her pussy. She prayed Samson would grant her an orgasm soon. She didn't care who gave it to her, as long as she got some relief.

A sudden swat that landed on both cheeks at the same time made her rock forward, moaning.

"Someone is having trouble concentrating," Samson stated. "I think it's time for you to remove your clothes so Rex will have better access. Stand up, sweetheart."

Charlotte held her breath while she concentrated on easing off the side of the platform. Her legs were wobbly, her bottom burning, her pussy pleading for attention.

When she met Samson's gaze, he had one brow lifted. "Clothes off. Fold them nicely in a pile here." He patted the spot next to him.

Her fingers were shaking as she untied her blouse and slid it off, folding it as well as she could before setting it on the platform. She unzipped the skirt next and stepped out of it, catching Rex's gaze.

He stood stoically across from her, his gaze on hers before sliding down her body. All the while, he tapped one palm with the paddle over and over as if impatient for her to finish.

She slipped off her shoes and then bent to remove her

socks. Lastly, she shrugged out of her thong, leaving herself completely naked for the first time in front of Rex.

She'd been naked in front of lots of people over the years. It was titillating. Rarely did it unnerve her. Tonight was one of those rare occasions. For some reason she badly wanted Rex to find her attractive. In fact, she let her gaze roam to the front of his jeans, hoping to see evidence of arousal.

Samson waved a hand in front of her, making her jolt in her spot and glance at him before lowering her gaze. "That's better. How about you worry about your own arousal instead of anyone else's?"

"Yes, Sir," she whispered, slightly mortified. Samson had never had to call her out on something like that. This was truly uncharted territory. And it wasn't Samson or Nile she was checking out. It was Rex. Another man. She didn't think Samson was mad, but she couldn't be sure. Part of her wished he would frown or show some sign it bothered him that she'd been checking out another man. His blasé attitude didn't go unnoticed.

Rex spoke next. "I want you on your back this time, spread eagle."

She crawled back onto the platform and lifted her arms above her head in a V. Samson still sat on the edge of the platform, now between her arms. She spread her legs wide next, keeping her gaze on the ceiling. Again, it didn't bother her a bit to be spread open for Rex. She prayed he liked what he saw. She didn't have any issues with self-esteem. Both Samson and Nile looked at her every day like she was the most beautiful creature on earth.

She closed her eyes and imagined what Rex was seeing so exposed to him for the first time. Creamy white skin. Freckles that dotted her nose and chest. Breasts that, although average in size, were pert. Pink nipples that stood at attention.

Between her legs were hairless swollen folds that at the moment had to be glistening with arousal.

When the paddle patted her belly, she sucked in a breath. It was one thing to have someone spank her backside. Though she'd witnessed others in similar situations, she didn't have much experience being flogged or paddled on her front.

Rex dragged the edge of the rubber along the bottom of her breasts, making her arch slightly. "Stay perfectly still, Charlotte," he reminded her in an authoritative, calm tone.

She shivered.

He flicked the tip of the paddle over her nipple.

She gasped as she tipped her head back, mouth falling open. If she opened her eyes, she would at least have a slight warning about his movements, but she found she liked not knowing.

Samson cupped her cheek from behind, his thumb gliding gently back and forth over her skin. "Deep breaths, sweetheart."

She inhaled slowly, but nearly jumped off the platform when Rex suddenly gave her pussy a light swat.

Rex tsked her. "We're just getting started, and already, you're struggling to obey."

"Sorry, Sir." Her words were breathy as she blinked up at Samson, trying desperately to center herself.

"Pretend your wrists and ankles are secured to the corners," Samson murmured, holding her gaze.

She nodded slightly. Naturally, the goal here was for her to break form, and she would, eventually, but she wanted to drag out the sweet torment as long as she could. The end result would be all the more delicious the longer she could hold out.

Rex tapped her thighs next, up and down the fronts and then in between. Each time he got close to her sex, she gritted her teeth against the need to react.

When his next tap landed on her nipple, she moaned. It

felt so damn good. One of the best feelings in the world. She'd never experienced anything quite like this. And Samson knew it.

Another gentle swat to her clit, immediately followed by the same nipple as a moment ago.

She gasped, suddenly close to coming. "Sir..." she murmured, her eyes on Samson.

He lifted a brow. "Not yet, sweetheart. Let Rex play."

He tapped the undersides of her breasts back and forth, making them jiggle with each impact. Another swat landed on her nipple next, harder. Intense. The sting was so good. When he did the same, only slightly firmer, to the other nipple, she couldn't stop her knees from drawing up slightly.

Samson gripped her chin. "Legs flat. You don't have permission to move."

She lowered them immediately.

Rex spoke again, his paddle tapping between her thighs. "How about if you lift these knees and spread them wide open."

She drew in a deep breath as she pulled her knees up and then opened herself up more intimately to his gaze.

When she heard the distinct tear of a condom wrapper, she tipped her gaze toward Rex, her heart racing at the thought that he might enter her. She was surprised Samson would grant that, especially so soon.

Instead of finding Rex with his jeans lowered and his cock in hand, she discovered he was lowering the condom down the handle of the paddle. *Holy shit.* He glanced at her. "Samson tells me you like having your pussy filled. I'm just getting prepared in case I need to give you a reminder about who's in charge here." He lifted a brow.

She swallowed, trying to decipher his words. When she glanced back at Samson, she knew exactly what the plan was, and the realization stopped her breath. There were differences between the way Samson and Nile played, and one of them was that Samson thoroughly enjoyed punishing her by driving her to the edge of an orgasm and leaving her there. She had no doubt he'd shared this information with Rex. Eventually, she would be impaled with that handle without permission to come.

Goose bumps rose on her arms.

Rex tapped her clit again, but he followed that with another spank to her nipple. The sting took her breath away as she hovered in that sweet spot between pleasure and pain, her favorite place on earth. All else disappeared when she went to this space.

Several more swats landed on her breasts, and then a hard spank to her clit again. She couldn't stop herself from reacting, her knees drawing together without permission.

Rex was suddenly kneeling on the platform, both hands on her legs, her thighs wider than she was capable of on her own, He held her like that for several seconds and then released one thigh to nudge the handle of his paddle at her entrance.

She held her breath as he toyed with her wetness, easing the handle into her in quick little spurts before thrusting it deep.

"Oh, God," she cried out.

Samson wrapped his hands around both her wrists and held her down, his lips coming to her neck to nibble until he reached her ear. "So gorgeous. Don't move."

She couldn't even breathe, let alone move. Her channel contracted around the handle of the paddle. She needed more. She needed Rex to move it in and out. She needed him to stroke her clit.

Her entire pussy throbbed.

And Samson continued to whisper sweetly in her ear. "You're doing great. I know how badly you need to come. Hold on to that. You don't have permission to orgasm yet."

She pursed her lips, fighting the urge to ignore him. She could do it. Come. Without anyone doing a single other thing. It didn't happen often, but occasionally she'd found herself so aroused she could come without being stroked anywhere at all.

Rex held the paddle with one hand. She could tell this without opening her eyes, based on the angle of the handle. When his other hand slid from her thigh to her belly, applying slight pressure that forced the hood fully away from her clit, she whimpered. "So pretty," he murmured. "Pink and swollen and wet with arousal."

She wanted to squirm, but knew that would only make things worse. Even though Samson had her hands, she had to concentrate to keep her knees high and parted. She started panting, fighting against the growing arousal.

Suddenly, Rex eased the handle nearly out of her and then thrust it back in.

She screamed.

"Music," Samson stated. "I love how you let everyone know when you're out of your mind with need."

When Rex did the same thing again, she bit into her bottom lip and held her breath.

Samson stroked her wrists with his thumbs, his lips tickling her neck. "If you can stay still for three more thrusts, Rex will let you come."

She gave a slight nod. There was no way she could speak. Instead she tried to focus on the backs of her eyelids.

Rex pulled the paddle completely out and then held her down while he eased it back in slowly. Torture. Heaven. Perfection. She needed to be permitted to come more than anything, but this was the BDSM she loved, the delicious ways she could be driven to the edge made her adrenaline pump.

Rex did the same thing again, but then he surprised her

with one last quick thrust, ending by tipping the handle up toward the front of her channel.

She gasped, her mouth falling open, but a second later he pinched her clit and commanded, "Come, Charlotte."

She shattered, her body pulsing everywhere as the orgasm shook her frame. Her clit thrummed between his thumb and finger because he didn't release her swollen nub while the orgasm consumed her.

It wasn't until she was fully sated that he released her clit and eased the paddle out of her. And then he reverently leaned over her pussy and kissed her lower lips. "Thank you. That was beautiful."

CHAPTER 14

Charlotte moaned into her pillow early the next morning when she heard Samson's phone ring. She tuned him out, too tired to move as he took the call and quietly headed for the bathroom.

The next thing she knew, the side of the bed dipped as Samson sat on the edge and leaned over her. "I'm so sorry, sweetheart, but I need to get back to Seattle."

She blinked her eyes open and rolled onto her back to look up at him, frowning. "What time is it?"

"Eight." He stroked her cheek. "There was some vandalism at the gym last night. My employees are meeting with the police, but I need to go assess the damage and deal with the mess."

"Shit. That's awful."

"Yeah. Looks like they were trying to break in and failed. Eventually the alarm went off, which probably sent them running from the scene, but not before breaking several windows and damaging the front doors."

She wiggled a hand out from under the blankets and

curled her fingers around his biceps. "Sorry. That sucks. You want me to go with you?"

He shook his head. "No. Stay. Deal with your business." He leaned over and kissed her forehead. When he drew back, his expression was serious. "Call Rex. Spend some time with him."

She swallowed. "Sir..." That was dangerous territory, and Samson knew it. After their scene last night, she'd been in a subspace that left her slightly drunk feeling from the submission and the orgasm. She'd curled up between them on a couch to recuperate while they'd spoken in hushed voices that she didn't even try to decipher.

He kissed her lips next, slowly. "Do it. You have a connection. Nile saw it. I saw it. Feel it out. If you don't, you'll never know, and neither of us wants that hanging over our relationship."

"But, Sir..." She gripped him tighter. Her heart was pounding and she was fully awake now. She also had no idea what to say. Was he pushing her away? Did he want her to pursue someone else? It was all too strange to fully wrap her mind around.

He smiled at her. "We adore you, sweetheart. You know that. But we would never hold you back from anything you want in life."

She fought against the tear that threatened in the corner of her eye as he stood, kissed her once more, and then left her alone in the hotel room.

She stared at the door in silence for a long time before that tear slid free and ran down the corner of her eye into her hair. She didn't swipe at it. This situation was so fucked up. How the hell had she managed to meet a third Dom who rocked her world?

Curling onto her side and drawing her knees up, she closed her eyes against the mental anguish.

You have two amazing Doms. Stop being so greedy.

She felt blindsided. After three years of bliss, during which she never once questioned her allegiance to Nile and Samson, she couldn't fathom how another Dom could step into her line of sight and capture her attention.

She needed a head exam. Nile and Samson adored her. They gave her everything she could ever want. She shouldn't crave more. It was all so illogical. Two men dominated her every day of her life. They did so every moment she was alone with them in their home. And yet, she'd been consumed with thoughts of another man for weeks. And it would seem her Doms were encouraging this. Was she some sort of sex addict?

She shook that last thought from her mind. It made no sense. This wasn't about sex. This was something else entirely. Sure, she had no doubt sex with Rex would rock her world, but the two of them clicked on another level. The same kind of connection she felt when she met Nile and then Samson. A fetish world kinship that was hard to find. One she'd managed to come upon and capture twice already. One she was coming to recognize had stepped into her path yet again.

Visions of Rex flashed through her mind like snapshots. The way he'd flogged her with such confidence and precision. The way he'd used his paddle so perfectly, seeming to know exactly how much pain she could take against her butt and then her most private areas. The way he'd held her chair out when they'd gone for coffee, ordered for her, looked her in the eye when she spoke. She remembered the nerves he exuded while they'd been in the coffee shop, nerves that contrasted with his total confidence in the club.

He was one of the good guys. She already had two of them.

Fisting her hands in her pillow, she rolled onto her belly again, feeling the way the sheets rubbed against every inch of her naked skin. After returning to the hotel room late last night, Samson had undressed her and tucked her into bed. She had fallen asleep when he'd slid in behind her and drew her tight against his chest. She could still feel his presence, smell his aftershave. If she reached out a hand, she would be able to touch the warmth he'd left behind.

She slid in and out of sleep, jolting awake each time as dreamland led her on a tortured path she could not shake. She was on her knees at the penthouse. Her hands were secured behind her back. Nile was tormenting her with a feather, trying to get her to squirm. Samson was waiting in front of her, flexing his palm, itching to spank her.

Rex was there too. He stood next to Samson with a flogger in each hand. Except they weren't normal floggers. Each strand of leather had sharp pointy tips on the ends. If he struck her with them, they would draw blood and cause undo pain. She couldn't see his face, so she wasn't sure if he was smiling or angry.

Finally, after an hour in and out of that horrible dream, she shoved from the bed and padded to the bathroom. After splashing water on her face, she met her gaze in the mirror. Her eyes looked sad and puffy. Her hair was a tangled mess hanging around her shoulders. When she glanced down at her nipples, she saw no remnants of last night's role play, but she knew if she touched them, they would be sore.

Forcing herself to get a grip, she turned around and flipped on the water in the shower. If she could wash away the last twelve hours, maybe she could get on with her day. It was only nine thirty. She didn't have plans to meet with her realtor until one, but she hoped a shower would make her feel less melancholy.

A sudden knock at the door made her jump in her spot. She spun around, thinking maybe housekeeping had her on their early rounds. She grabbed a towel from the rack, wrapped it around her, and padded across the room.

A quick look through the peephole made her gasp. She didn't hesitate to open the door. "Rex?"

He held up a tray that held two steaming cups and offered her a crooked grin. "Brought you coffee."

She held the towel closed with a palm between her breasts, still blinking at him in confusion.

He lifted a brow as he lowered his arm. "Can I come in?"

"Samson had to leave," she responded, as if that were somehow relevant when she knew it was not.

Rex nodded. "I know that. He called me."

She narrowed her gaze. "Did he ask you to come here?"

"Yes."

A long exhale left her lungs. *Why?* She was so confused. Not for the first time since she'd entered this weird new world, she wondered if perhaps Samson was tired of her and was hoping he might be able to pawn her off on a new Dom.

That didn't explain Nile's equally weird participation, but maybe he agreed. Her mouth went dry.

"Charlotte?"

She jerked her gaze back to Rex, swallowing back emotion. Finally, she realized she needed to step back and let him in. "Sorry, Sir," she murmured, automatically slipping into a submissive role as he stepped over the threshold. It was ingrained in her to submit to a Dom when he was in her private space, be that her home or a hotel room.

Rex eased the door shut behind him and then lifted her chin with a finger. "Relax. You're not submitting to me right now." He glanced toward the bathroom. "Were you about to shower?"

"Yes…" The word fell off as she forced herself not to add *Sir*. It wasn't like she submitted to every man who came to her home or hotel, but she was accustomed to doing it with Samson and Nile, and now apparently Rex.

He sighed. "Okay, let's do it this way. You'll submit to me

just long enough to get showered and dressed and get out of here, then we'll go have breakfast as equals. Will that work?"

"Yes, Sir." She squeezed the towel, her legs trembling as her body reacted to him in ways she simply couldn't fully explain. Her stiff nipples rubbed against the terry cloth. Wetness pooled between her legs.

He nodded toward the bathroom. "Come on."

She followed him, dutifully, just like she would Nile or Samson.

He set the coffee on the vanity and turned to face her. The room was filled with steam. "Give me the towel." He held out a hand.

She obediently uncurled her fingers and released the soft material, holding it out to him. Left naked, she shivered, but didn't cover herself. He'd seen her just as naked only a few hours ago. *But not without Samson.*

Rex cupped one breast and looked at it closely. When he released it, he motioned for her to spin around.

She hurried to do so, trembling as he stroked a few fingers down her back and over her butt.

"Good. I wanted to make sure you didn't have any lasting marks. Your skin is so damn sensitive. I never want to injure you."

Ah, that made sense. He was just ensuring he hadn't struck her too hard last night.

"Get in the shower, Charlotte."

Her hand shook as she opened the enclosure and stepped inside. The steamed glass door afforded her some protection against his wandering gaze. Not that she minded him looking at her. She liked it. A lot. But this entire situation unnerved her.

She took deep breaths while she shampooed and then conditioned her hair. There was no way she was going to risk shaving with her hands so unsteady, so she skipped that part and hurried to use the body wash next. After rinsing, she turned off the water and opened the door.

Rex held out her towel with both hands. He wrapped it around her and patted her dry, making her feel pampered and cared for. "Sit." He pointed at the toilet seat after tucking the towel under her arms.

She gladly lowered to sitting, watching him as he found her brush on the sink. She continued to watch him in the mirror as he gently worked out the tangles and then set the brush down. "It's cold outside. Can I blow it dry?"

She nodded, biting into her bottom lip. "Thank you, Sir."

He smiled and then picked up the hairdryer. As if he were a beautician, he expertly fluffed her hair with one hand while drying it with the other. It would be left with perfect waves when he was done. She took the time to close her eyes and try to control her beating heart.

Rex was here. In her hotel room. Taking care of her. The room she'd slept in last night with Samson. The room where she'd cried earlier from confusion.

She was even more confused than ever now, but at the same time soothed by the way he handled her. How was she supposed to reconcile all these feelings?

When he finished, he helped her stand. "Get dressed." He handed her the coffee. It would be cool enough by now to drink, and she desperately needed a long deep drink of caffeine.

She sighed as she took two more sips. A latte, exactly how she liked it. "Thank you, Sir."

Back in the room, Rex took a seat in the room's only armchair and casually crossed one ankle over his other knee as he sat back to drink his own coffee.

Charlotte set hers on the bedside table and turned to rummage through the top drawer under the television, trying to think about what she might want to wear this morning.

With Rex watching her, she grabbed a matching black thong and bra set, a pair of designer jeans, and a black fitted turtleneck. She dressed quickly and then added short black ankle boots and a thick multi-colored cardigan that hung down to her knees.

"I'm just going to finish up in the bathroom, okay, Sir?" she asked before leaving the room.

He nodded. "Of course. Take your time."

She didn't close the door as she applied minimal makeup and then made sure her hair wasn't out of control. When she returned, she added several pieces of jewelry from the nightstand. "I'm ready, Sir."

Rex pushed to standing and came toward her. He set his hands on her arms and ran them up to cup her face, tipping her chin back so she met his gaze. "You're stunning in all forms. Naked. Disheveled. Makeup-less. Wet. Dry. Made up. Clothed." He smiled and then stroked her cheeks. "Let's get out of here before I ravage you."

His words eased her tension. She took a deep breath, and opened the door. During the ride down the elevator to the lobby, they stood close to each other but didn't speak. As soon as they stepped out of the building, she felt a strange weight lift off her.

As she released a long breath, Rex set a hand on her lower back and smiled down at her. "Feel better now?"

She nodded. "Much. Thank you. Sorry about that. It's... hard to explain."

"I know the perfect place to get brunch. Let's go get settled, and then you can explain it to me."

Charlotte wasn't at all sure she could explain anything to him. Her entire world felt like it was upside down, sideways, and spinning out of control. And here she was walking down the sidewalk in Denver with a man who was not one of her Doms, heading to breakfast.

It was impossible to ignore that everyone around them was smiling and happy. After all, the holidays did that to people. It was a weekend. They were probably out shopping. Decorations were hung from the lampposts and could be seen in every storefront. It was soothing.

Rex was a perfect gentleman. He ensured she walked on the side away from the street, guided her around objects and people, and opened the door when they reached the restaurant.

By the time they were seated in a far corner of the upscale place, cloth napkins in their laps, water poured, and a coffee pot on the table, she decided she'd stepped out of the real world and into a different dimension.

"Are you usually a breakfast person?" Rex asked.

"Yes. When I have time. I'm not a morning person at all, so sometimes I'm running too late to stop and eat. Those days I end up with a granola bar during the commute."

"Well, not today. We have plenty of time. Pick out something ridiculous and we'll take our time."

She loved that plan, and smiled at him for a long while before lowering her gaze and quickly deciding on an omelet meal with far too many sides. They gave their orders to the waiter and then she took a fortifying sip of coffee.

Rex set his elbows on the table and steepled his fingers. "I don't want you to be nervous with me."

She chuckled. "Well, that ship sailed about two seconds after I met you."

"In high school or two weeks ago?" he teased.

She couldn't help it. He made her giggle. "Honestly, probably in high school too. You were so...knowledgeable. I couldn't compete with that. I felt like I was some kind of alien being when you tried to explain physics to me."

He frowned. "I never meant to make you feel that way."

She waved a hand through the air. "Oh, don't even worry.

You couldn't help it. You were a genius. Still are." She sobered and leaned closer. "Only now I know you're a genius in several ways I hadn't imagined."

Rex smirked and then ran a hand down his face. "I'm nervous with you too. It's hard to avoid."

"Not when we're in the club, though. Not when I'm submitting to you," she pointed out.

He nodded. "It's true. I have difference facets of my personality. And to be honest, I've mostly kept them separated. I haven't been in any long-term relationships with anyone outside of Zodiac. Meeting someone I dominated for coffee or breakfast is unusual for me. It's like an odd mixed world where I'm not completely dominant in the moment, but not as awkward as I tend to be either." He gave a wry smile. "As you well know, I'm a nerd at heart. I can put that aside and be a totally different person when I'm dominating, but when I'm not... I'm out of sorts, I suppose."

"And it's intriguing, so don't think I'm bothered by it."

He nodded slowly, seeming to watch her to ensure she wasn't feeding him a line.

The waiter arrived at that moment and set their food in front of them. "Let me know if you need anything else," he stated as he left them to enjoy the meal.

"Wow, this is a lot of food," Charlotte pointed out.

Rex took a bite of his pancakes and moaned softly. "God, I love pancakes. I never eat them, but then I remember I love them."

"Nile makes amazing pancakes," she said before she could stop herself. Now probably wasn't the ideal time to discuss one of her Doms.

"He's a chef, right? I bet he makes all sorts of fantastic meals. Does he cook for you every day?"

Okay, so we are going down this path. She shook her head. "Nope. I wish. He's not usually home in the evening. Hell, the three of us are rarely all in the house at the same time. Often only one of us is home in the evening. We all have demanding jobs."

"Sounds like it. Tell me about them." He took another bite, holding her gaze.

"You really want to talk about Samson and Nile?"

"Yes. They are important to you. I want to hear about them."

She glanced down at her plate and then forked a bite of omelet and enjoyed it while considering what she wanted to say.

Rex sipped his coffee and then held up a hand. "Wait. First explain to me what happened in your hotel this morning."

"Yeah, hmmm. That's difficult to dissect. I'm not entirely sure. I can tell you that when I'm in our home, our arrangement is that I submit to Samson and Nile at all times. It's ingrained in me. The term 'home' easily gets transferred to hotels when I'm out of town."

"I get that. But do you submit to every human who enters your house?"

She sighed, her shoulders dropping. That was the clencher here. "No."

"And yet…"

"Yeah, you're not like other people. I can't even say it's because I've submitted to you at Zodiac because that makes no sense either. We've had guests over many times, some of whom I've submitted to in the past. I don't submit to them. I'm unnerved by my reaction to you this morning." She shuddered and then wrapped her fingers around her mug of coffee to steady herself.

Rex reached out a hand and set it on her wrist. "Don't worry. I'm sure it's no big deal."

Except it was a huge deal. To her. There was no

explanation for her reaction to his arrival. On top of that, she'd enjoyed his dominance this morning immensely.

"Let's back up," he urged. "Tell me more about your dynamic with Samson and Nile."

She finished another bite and then met his gaze. "We have an agreement. I adore them both. They treat me like a queen." Those words sounded slightly forced to her under the current circumstances.

"I can understand why."

She flushed.

"No, really. You command respect. You're not a pushover. You're strong and powerful and commanding in your own right. I'm sure your business runs like a well-tuned machine."

She shrugged.

"See? I know I'm right. I'm sure you're well aware that you're not alone. Millions of people in powerful positions with lots of responsibility like to leave all that at the door at the end of the day and turn the power over to someone else."

Charlotte nodded. "Of course. I totally get that. I even understand it's become habitual for me to submit to them as soon as I walk through the front door. It's like I remove not only my clothes, but my problems as well."

Rex watched her closely while she spoke, slowly working his way through the plate of food in front of him at the same time.

She took a few more bites while pondering what she'd just told him. Finally, she dropped her fork, wiped her lips, and sat back. "What I don't understand is why I've suddenly got an itch that won't go away. I have the best life. Two men adore me. They offer very different types of dominance. I've been the happiest of any point in my life since we moved in together. Why on earth would I suddenly do a double take when another man walks by?"

"Me?" he stated.

"Yes."

He swallowed and set his fork down too. "Listen, I didn't mean to cause stress in your life. It was never my intention. I had no idea who Colin had arranged for me to dominate that first night. I was just as surprised as you." His voice lowered. "And equally shocked at the connection we have. I love spending time with you. In and out of the club. Watching you come like that last night will forever be imbedded as one of my fondest memories."

She smiled. "It was pretty awesome."

"I would never trade it for the world, but I don't want to cause you such consternation either. I feel like you're stuck in some strange limbo, as if I'm trying out to replace the Doms in your life. And I'm not going to lie. I'd give almost anything to have you be mine, but I would never poach another Dom's submissive. *Never*. I spent half the night pacing my house, reminding myself what we did last night was too intense. It wasn't just a scene. I knew I felt more for you than appropriate. I need to back off."

"But you're here," she whispered, uncertain if she was glad or not. Of course she was ecstatic to spend more time with him. But was this wise? Perhaps he as right.

"Yeah, I'm here. I didn't show up without specific urging from Samson though. Now I'm trying to figure out why a man who so obviously adores you and would move the moon over if he thought you needed it, would call me this morning and ask me to go pick you up and spend time with you."

She took a deep breath. "I think he's pushing me to confront whatever this is. In his mind, we have an agreement and nothing else. He doesn't own me. Neither does Nile. We made a mutually beneficial arrangement under the guise that it could be broken by any one of us if we ever wanted out. There is nothing legally binding between us. No two of us are married."

"You speak as if you three exist to scratch each other's itches, and I know that's far from true. I've seen how they look at you and you them. Your arrangement may have started out as something lighter and less committed, but it's evolved into what it is today, and that's something huge."

"You might be right, but Samson and Nile are adamant about me exploring this thing." She waved a hand back and forth between them. "They might not like it, but they're going at this from the stance that they have always been willing to set me free if the time came."

"Doesn't that infuriate you just a little?"

She flinched, glancing down at the table.

"Yeah. That's what I thought. You're in a loving, doting relationship. It has to hurt that they're encouraging you to explore outside your arrangement."

She chewed on her bottom lip for a moment and then released it, knowing his words rang true. "That thought has crossed my mind. I keep reminding myself they're simply being open."

"I'm a pretty open guy myself, but I wouldn't give my woman permission to sleep around."

She lifted a finger to make a point. "And they certainly haven't given me that right either. I would never do something they didn't expressly permit, and sex with another man would be crossing the line." Who was she trying to convince? Him or herself?

He leaned closer. "I didn't mean to imply you would break their trust, Charlotte. I'm just trying to figure out what's happening here."

"I know you are. I don't mean to sound defensive. I'm just sort of out of body I guess. I've never once come upon a Dom I fell into sync with so precisely since moving in with Samson and Nile. It's...strange, and I can't make sense of it in my head."

He reached across the table and took both of her hands in his. "I hate that I might inadvertently be making it harder for you. I had completely convinced myself to bow out when Samson called me this morning. Curiosity caused me to come to you. It wasn't helpful. Not for either of us. I really think it would be best if I took a step back and left you alone. You're in a fantastic committed relationship. I can't see any reason in the world why you would leave it. I can't stand the idea that I'm responsible for you second guessing yourself. I won't be that guy." He gave both of her hands a tight squeeze and then released them. "Besides, although it was fun working with Samson last night and Nile two weeks ago, I've never been the kind of guy who would enjoy sharing a partner. I've always thought it was fine for a scene, but not in the long run. I've considered myself a one-woman man who would eventually meet someone to spend my life with. I kind of hoped she would be both available and make my blood boil like you do."

A giant lump formed in her throat. She understood what he was saying, but she hated his words all the same.

He shook his head slightly. "The truth is, you've expanded my vision and made me think. So, I'm going through a stage of confusion myself. Sharing you with Nile and then with Samson wasn't simply clinical for me. Feelings got involved. My foundation is shaken a bit at the realization that I wasn't bothered by it. In fact, I enjoyed it immensely. Sharing the dominance opens up a whole new world of possibility. I have a lot to consider."

She watched him while he spoke. He met her gaze several times, but he also fidgeted with his napkin and flipped his fork around several times.

He sighed. "The reality is that I have stuff to work through, and you need to face your situation head-on. Ask yourself why you're interested in someone else. Confront Nile and Samson. Talk it out."

She bit into her lower lip and nodded. God, he was so right. She should feel elated to have him spell it out so plainly.

"Let me walk you back to your hotel. I know you have an appointment this afternoon with your realtor. You need some time to regroup. We don't really know each other that well. There's no sense in this weird connection getting in the way of your life." He shrugged as if this was no big deal.

Maybe it is no big deal.

"We have some mutual history. We did a few scenes. You enjoy my style of dominance. I enjoy your style of submission. It's not that unusual. It's time to stop before someone gets hurt."

She nodded, fighting the urge to disagree with him. In reality, he was giving her a speech she should have had the balls to give herself. Break this off before someone got hurt.

Rex dropped several bills on the table, pushed to standing, and then helped her do the same. He kept a hand on the small of her back as he led her from the restaurant.

She couldn't speak. There were no words anyway. He'd said them all perfectly.

The short walk was awkward, and Charlotte's mood didn't match the holiday excitement all around her. People were smiling and laughing. Happy holiday music wafted from every open door. The sound of bells suddenly annoyed her.

When they arrived back at her hotel room, she opened the door with her keycard and glanced at him, knowing he wouldn't come inside. That was beyond dangerous territory.

He grabbed her shoulders and pulled her into his chest, kissing her forehead. "You have a fantastic life. Enjoy it." He leaned back and offered her a wan smile.

She swallowed, trying so hard to find words that wouldn't come. It's like he kept stealing them from her. "Rex…"

"I know, Charlotte. I know. It's going to be okay. Go on.

Get inside. I hope you find the perfect location for your boutique. I'll be sending good vibes."

She backed into the hotel room, still staring at him as the door shut, breaking the contact. She would need good vibes. That was for sure. But she wasn't at all certain it was a good idea to open a branch of her boutique in Denver, Colorado. The entire city would forever remind her of Rex.

She forced herself not to cry as she backed up and flopped down on top of the mattress. She didn't even remove her clothes. Who would know? Who would see? At the moment, she didn't care.

CHAPTER 15

Charlotte was unable to focus on the properties her realtor had lined up for her. She'd lost interest, her mind wandering. There was no way she would be able to concentrate enough to care about securing a property, so rather than waste her realtor's time, she offered an excuse that she suddenly needed to be back in Seattle and left a day early.

When she arrived Sunday night, she was exhausted and relieved no one was home. The penthouse was quiet, but she still went through the motions of removing her clothes and switching to a robe. She was chilled, so she chose a thick, fleece robe that still didn't warm her up.

She padded to the kitchen and opened the fridge, but nothing appealed to her. Finally, she sighed, and decided what she really needed was sleep. The work week was going to be very busy. It would keep her mind off her problems. She still hadn't done nearly enough Christmas shopping either. Perhaps if she forced herself to get in the holiday spirit and find some gifts for her Doms, she would snap out of it.

She headed for her own room, dropped the robe, and slid between the sheets, praying her mind would slow down and let her rest. Relationships went through ups and downs. Hers was just in a slump, right? The fact that Samson had encouraged Rex to come to her hotel room yesterday really bothered her.

And Nile had said nothing. Her conversations with the two of them Saturday night and earlier this morning had been clipped. Neither man dominated her. Everything was a mess. She hated it.

Charlotte fell asleep, but flipped around fitfully during the night, aware that Nile and Samson also hadn't come to her when they got home. She thought she'd heard the door creak open a few times, but no one entered.

What a cluster. If she had any idea how to fix this situation, she would, but she knew deep down she was at least half the problem, and discussing it wouldn't help. She needed to figure her shit out and get her head straight. ASAP.

Samson slid into the booth across from Nile and plopped heavily onto his ass. He rubbed his forehead, fighting the headache that wouldn't quite go away.

"Thanks for meeting me. I know your day is jammed," Nile said, nudging Samson's leg with his own.

"Yeah. Yours is too. This is important though. We have to talk." Samson sat forward. "It's been a week. She's distant and clearly unsettled. We have to do something." He'd been watching her closely every day since she returned from Denver. She wasn't herself.

"I know she had breakfast with Rex after you left, Saturday, but it would seem they agreed not to see each other again and haven't even spoken. I'm worried her motives were misguided."

Samson sighed and glanced around. Even though this

diner was usually one of his go-to locations when two of them had a chance to grab a bite to eat in the middle of the day, for some reason the place was annoying him today. Too much Christmas—lights, music, decorations. He wasn't feeling the happiness. "I agree. Obviously the two of them connected in some way, and she's not handling it well."

"I'm positive her reasoning has to do with us, and though I hate to admit it out loud, we have to face that fact that we may have lost her." Nile rubbed his eyes with his thumb and middle finger.

Samson ran a hand down his face and slouched in his seat, gaze on the table. "Yes." He hadn't seen this coming. The three of them had been so happy for so long without anything tipping their ship that he'd assumed they would be together for the long haul. Granted, maybe it was his own damn fault for never specifically telling Charlotte, or Nile for that matter, how he felt about them. None of them had ever used the L word. Perhaps they should have.

"It's not simple," Nile continued. "Losing her affects three people. Every time I consider a life without her, I choke up. I'm not eating or sleeping well."

Samson lifted his gaze to find Nile looking right at him. He swallowed through the emotional lump in his throat. "I know." He even reached across the table and gave Nile's hand a squeeze. They weren't overly affectionate with each other often, but Samson had a special bond with Nile that would also be sorely missed if this thing went to shit.

They held each other's gazes for several moments.

Finally, Samson cleared his throat. "I know we don't express ourselves in words often, but I won't let her walk away without making sure she knows I love her. And...the same goes for you." It was as close as he could come to telling the man across from him how he felt at the moment.

Nile gave a wan smile. "Ditto." He sucked in a long breath.

"So, we face her. Tell her how we feel and let her go. It's cliché, but we don't have another choice. Whatever is going on with her, it didn't disappear just because she told Rex she didn't want to see him anymore. She has to figure this out, and we have to be prepared to lose her."

Samson nodded, his gaze dropping again. He couldn't fathom what life would look like without her. It was unimaginable and made his stomach clench. When the waitress came by, all he ordered was coffee. It was all Nile had in front of him also.

How did their lives veer so off track?

Samson felt like he was partially to blame. They hadn't checked in with her often enough. Made sure she was happy. Renegotiated. Took a pulse. It was an important part of the lifestyle, and they'd all ignored it.

On the other hand, it was possible that no matter what any of them had done or said, Charlotte still might have taken one look at Rex and felt a connection with him she was somehow missing in her life. It happened all the time. Now Samson just had to figure out how to face this issue head on with minimal damage.

"Let's talk to her tonight."

Samson was pacing the kitchen that evening while Nile cooked. When they heard the front door open and shut, they paused and glanced at each other.

Ordinarily, one of them would go to her when she came home. Neither of them moved. She would seek them out in the kitchen in a few minutes. It seemed wrong to confront her while she undressed at the front door.

On top of the obvious strain on their relationship, none of them had had sex in the past week either. That was unheard of. Rarely did a day go by when either Rex or Samson or both of them together didn't rock her world.

Of course, normally Charlotte was amorous and made it impossible to deny her. She hadn't been since she returned from Denver.

When she rounded the corner and stepped into the kitchen, she glanced at first Samson and then Nile. "Did I miss something, Sirs?"

Samson realized they were both still standing frozen in their spots, waiting for her. He reached out a hand. "Come here, sweetheart."

She shuffled forward, but she looked skeptical.

"We need to talk," Samson continued.

She licked her lips. "Yeah. Look, I know I've been preoccupied. I'm sorry about that. I've been super busy. The stores are crazy with the holiday shoppers. I keep worrying I didn't order enough. I'll pull it back together soon."

Samson hauled her into his embrace as soon as she was close enough. He hugged her tight against his chest, loving the feel of her warmth, something he'd taken for granted for far too long. He inhaled the vanilla scent of her hair and threaded his fingers into the thickness at the back of her neck.

He glanced over her shoulder at Nile as his other partner joined them. Nile cocooned her from her back, his arms snaking in around Samson's.

For a moment they just rocked together like this. Content while at the same time putting off the inevitable.

When Nile drew back, his hands still on her shoulders, Samson tipped her away from him and met her gaze. "Nile and I talked earlier. We think you need to take some time to explore other options. You're obviously not happy. It might help if you moved out of the penthouse and spent some time sorting things out." He nearly choked on the words, but they needed to be said. He needed to set her free instead of waiting for things to go bad between them.

Her eyes went wide and her mouth fell open.

"He's right," Nile stated behind her, making her spin his direction. "If you love someone, set them free and all that." He forced a smile.

Charlotte flinched, and then shook her head. She jerked out of their grasp and backed up a few steps. "Are you serious? I know we've got some stuff to discuss, but I didn't realize you wanted me to move out. Who are you doing this for? Me or yourselves?" She glanced back and forth between them. Before either of them had a chance to respond, she continued. "I mean, while I've been grappling with my own issues, it hasn't escaped my attention that both of you have been tiptoeing around me for weeks." Her bottom lip was shaking.

Samson shook his head, surprised at her reaction. "No. God, no. You've misread us. We're working our asses off to make sure you have what you need."

"It's a bit too convenient," she added as she swiped at tears before crossing her arms and hugging herself. "We don't have a commitment between us. We never have. But you're talking like we're just three people scratching an itch, and it suddenly feels like you two have ganged up on me and plotted to end it." She lifted a shoulder to wipe at another tear in the corner of her eye.

Samson gasped and then rubbed a hand down his face, glancing at Nile to see if the man had anything to add that might fix this.

Nile took a step forward, shaking his head. "God, Charlotte. You've totally misread this. It's not like that at all."

"Really?" she asked, sarcastically. "Then enlighten me. What is it like?"

Nile glanced at Samson and then licked his lips. "We love you. So much it hurts."

Her mouth fell open, her eyes wide, as she stared at Nile and then switched her gaze to Samson.

"He's right. We've been completely remiss in expressing our feelings. Both of us. I take full responsibility for my part. I've known I've been in love with you for nearly three years. I have no idea why I never said anything. It caused you to think this arrangement didn't mean anything to me when it really means the world."

Nile spoke again. "We haven't been able to sleep this entire week worrying about what you're thinking. It never crossed my mind that you thought we were trying to break up with you. I'd give anything to keep you. We both would."

Samson set a hand on Nile's shoulder and drew him closer. "We're a unit. All three of us. I love both of you, and I'm so sorry I never said it before now."

"That being said, we get that you're having doubts and need some time. We won't hold you back from whatever you need. Like Samson said, you should spend some time alone. Maybe this isn't right for you anymore."

She shook her head violently, shocking Samson. "No. Jesus. I'm not leaving the two of you." Tears fell down her cheeks and she swiped at them with her fingers. "I love you both so much. I can't even believe none of us ever said anything. This relationship is my life. I won't give it up. I don't understand what's crawled up my ass and shaken my foundation, but it didn't replace how I feel about you two. I'm still crazy about you. Just confused at the same time. I know that must sound absurd, but it's true."

Samson drew in a slow breath, taking the time to consider her words. "Okay, so you're polyamorous, and you like new sexual experiences. That's not really a shocker, sweetheart. Maybe you're just not the sort of person who wants to spend her life tied down to any one or even two men."

She swallowed and dipped her head. "That makes me feel awful."

Nile grabbed her around the waist and hauled her into his side, tipping her head back. "Don't. It's just who you are." He smiled. "Lucky for you, we're accommodating. If you need other people to join us, we'll deal with it." He shrugged. "Hell, we both like Rex. We both clicked with him. Maybe we just need to invite him to explore joining us."

She shook her head. "I don't see that working. He's dealing with his own issues too. He's never shared someone before, not like this, not full-time."

"He shared just fine last weekend," Samson pointed out.

"That was a scene. Not real life."

"Was it though? It felt real to me."

She leaned her head on Nile's chest and fisted her hand in his shirt. "Forget Rex. I'm more worried about the fact that another Dom was able to catch my attention. What the hell is wrong with me that I can't be satisfied with two men?"

Samson forced a slight chuckle. "Nothing's wrong with you. You are who you are, and neither of us is going to take that away from you."

"I'm never leaving you two. I meant what I said. I love you both. I just need to get over myself and remember who I belong to—two men who adore me and remind me every day and give me everything."

Samson ran a palm up and down her back, finally clasping Nile's hand behind her. "Okay, but hear me out. Plan B. You obviously need more. At the very least scenes with other Doms and permission to act on them. We'll renegotiate our open door policy and figure out what works for you. Maybe you didn't realize you needed more, but you obviously do. So, it's time to sit down and spend a few hours creating a life that gives you more fulfillment."

She tipped her head back and glanced between them again. "That sounds incredibly one-sided and greedy of me."

Nile shook his head. "Not at all. If it's who you are, then you can't help that. If you truly believe you want to remain in this relationship, then we're both secure enough to work out a plan that will make you happier."

She cried again, uglier this time, sucking in sobs.

Samson closed the distance, flattening his chest to her side so closely that his face was inches from Nile.

Nile reached up with his free hand and cupped the back of Samson's head. They met and held gazes, both of them smiling. "We've got this," Nile said to the room at large, his gaze still on Samson's. "I love you both."

"I love you both too," Samson managed to murmur. It was strange how much easier it was to say those words after all these years of thinking he might ruin what they had if he crossed that line.

CHAPTER 16

Rex could not believe he was doing this. He paced the lobby of the address Samson had given him, running a hand through his hair several times. This seemed like the worst idea known to man.

On top of his extreme apprehension about how he was going to feel following Samson's suggestion, he wasn't at all sure it was a good idea to blindside Charlotte.

And on Christmas Eve.

Yep. Dropping everything and flying to Seattle for some crazy plan of Nile and Samson's on the day before Christmas showed a ridiculous lack of forethought. There was a chance Charlotte would slam the door in his face and tell him to get lost.

Samson didn't seem to think that would be the case, however. According to him, Charlotte was far less conflicted than she'd believed. All she needed was the opportunity to experiment with her polyamory.

So, Rex was now in Seattle like a lovesick puppy. If he'd had a tail, it would be wagging at the thought of seeing her again.

"Hey."

He spun around to find Nile exiting the elevator. He extended a hand. "So glad you came."

"I'm nowhere near as confident as you about the wisdom of your plan," he returned as he shook Nile's hand.

Nile smiled. "Trust us. Just open your mind to the possibility."

Rex shuddered. "Look, I'm not remotely opposed to your lifestyle. I get it. I have numerous friends who live in polyamorous relationships. I'm not judging anyone. But this is all new to me, so I'm nervous."

"You shared Charlotte with both of us on two occasions. You said yourself you enjoyed both scenes and felt comfortable. This is no different."

Rex shook his head. "This is totally different. You're asking me to come into your home and join a three-year scene already in progress."

Nile took a deep breath. "I hear you. And if this doesn't feel right after a few days or a week, you can always go back to your apartment in Denver. All of us will be far more informed about ourselves. No harm done."

Rex disagreed with Nile's assessment. A lot of harm could be done in a few days. Especially to himself. He could fall even more head over heels with Charlotte who in the end would stay with her current Doms and tell him to take a hike. It was going to hurt beyond measure.

The only reason he was standing here was because he would do anything for Charlotte, including give her this experience. He was still wrapping his head around entering a polyam relationship, but he was equally aware that his life had sucked since he last spoke to her. No way would he turn down an offer to come stay in her home, even if the thought emotionally drained him. Even a single moment with her will have been worth it.

Explaining to his parents that he would be spending Christmas in Seattle with friends had been a challenge. They'd been shocked and disappointed, but he'd spent the day before with them, and his mother had surprised him with a full Christmas dinner as if the twenty-third were the new holiday.

Nile led Rex to the elevator. "I'll have the doorman get your information down and give you an access key tomorrow." He pushed the button for the penthouse, making Rex nearly as nervous about where they lived as he was about who lived there.

He made amazing money, mostly because he was good at his job and everyone knew it. He could out-hack any person he'd ever met, breaking into even the tightest systems. His bosses knew it. They compensated him well to ensure he didn't leave.

However, he was still a frugal person. He only had what he needed. The rest had been going into a retirement fund for several years.

As the elevator rose, he wiped his palms on his dark navy jeans. *Please God let this be a good surprise for Charlotte.* The last thing he wanted was to inadvertently make her Christmas uncomfortable. Rex licked his lips. "I know Charlotte's mom moved to Florida, but don't you and Samson have families that expect you at the holidays? How do you explain this arrangement to them?"

Nile smiled at him. "Samson's parents are both deceased. He has extended family he visits in the summer. Each year they beg him to join them for the holidays, but he turns them down. My father is still living, but he's remarried, and he and his wife are currently traveling through Europe."

Rex took a deep breath. At least he didn't have to meet anyone's parents today. That would push him over the edge.

When the elevator door slid open, he found himself stepping directly into their home. He hadn't considered that, expecting a hallway. Instead, Nile was already taking Rex's suitcase and pushing it aside while Rex removed his coat.

"That was fast," Charlotte called from somewhere deeper in the house.

Nile whispered, "I told her I was meeting a delivery guy downstairs." He nodded toward the numerous boxes stacked around the entryway. "We haven't had a chance to decorate for Christmas. We were planning to do so tonight. She thinks I met someone downstairs about a tree. It's actually already in here." He pointed at an enormous box among the others.

Rex was beyond nervous as he followed Nile down a short hallway that led from the front door. A few seconds later, they stepped into an enormous great room that included a giant sectional on the right facing a fireplace and a flat screen.

To the left was a kitchen area with dark wood cabinets and counters.

Charlotte was seated on the sectional, curled up on one end, her back to him, her head buried in a book. He could only see the back of her, but her gorgeous hair made his breath hitch already, and the edge of a bright-red silk robe made his cock twitch. She hadn't moved yet.

Samson was across from her, his phone in his hand. He was pretending to examine it, but his eyes were lifted and his mouth curled up into a smile.

Suddenly, Charlotte lifted her gaze and twisted her neck around, speaking at the same time. "Nile?" The second she spotted Rex, her gorgeous green eyes widened, and her lips parted. She blinked several times.

To Rex, she was a sight for sore eyes. Even curled up on the couch, a blanket tucked around her, hair piled on top of her head, no makeup. God, she was gorgeous.

And then her face lit up and she jumped to her feet, the blanket falling to the floor, leaving her in the deep red robe that reached just below her butt and was tied loose enough in front to reveal deep cleavage. "Rex?" She glanced from him to Nile to Samson behind her. "What the...?"

Samson stood and came up behind her. "Merry Christmas, sweetheart." He ran his hands up and down her arms and kissed her neck.

Her hand came to her mouth as she continued to look stunned.

Nile slapped a hand on Rex's back and continued farther into the room. "We didn't think you would mind if we invited Rex for the holidays."

Charlotte's hand dropped and she smiled wide. "Not at all. How did you manage to arrange this?" Her gaze was on Rex.

He finally came more fully into the room, nervous, but growing more comfortable. At least she didn't seem pissed. "It took some convincing," he began. "Your Doms are very persuasive when they put their minds to it."

"Don't I know it."

Samson cleared his throat behind her and tipped her chin back to meet her gaze from over the top of her head. "No one gave you permission to break your role. I get you're shocked, but add a bit of respect and submission to your surprise." He lifted a brow.

Rex couldn't help but smile. The man had such an authoritative way about him.

"Yes, Sir," Charlotte responded, her gaze coming back to Rex when Samson released her chin. "Would you like to sit down, Sir?" She pointed at the sectional. It was big enough for about eight people to lounge without touching each other. At the moment, Rex wanted to touch her.

He circled the end of the sofa and stepped into her space, knowing he had been granted every liberty for this stay. In order to let her know exactly where he stood right off the bat, he didn't hesitate to cup the chin Samson had just released and angle it toward him this time. He set a hand on her belly, his fingers grazing Samson's forearm, and slid it up to cup the underside of her breast.

When she gasped, he kissed her lips gently before pulling back. "I heard you might like to experiment with having another Dom in the house."

She licked her lips and nodded absently. "I wouldn't turn it down, Sir," she murmured.

He eased his hand up farther and flicked his thumb over her already stiff nipple, enjoying the glide of his hand over the silk barrier. Perhaps it should have been uncomfortable taking such liberties with her while Samson also held her from the other side, but it wasn't as awkward as he would have expected.

He'd spoken several times with both Nile and Samson, once in a group conversation in the past week. They had explained where they stood and that they wanted Charlotte to have every experience that made her happy. They'd made it very clear that if Rex came to stay with them for a week, he would have the same access to her as they both did.

Someone needed to tell Charlotte the plan before Rex took this any further. She was still shocked, and hadn't consented to adding Rex to the home. "Do you mind if I stay for a few days?"

"I'd like that, Sir." She held his gaze.

"I have some vacation time, but I can also work from here," he informed her. Samson and Nile had made it clear he was welcome to stay as long as everyone was still on the same page. If that was a week, great. If it lasted longer, they could reevaluate.

Apparently, Charlotte's Doms had not misjudged her, based on her reaction to Rex's arrival. However, no matter how hot she made him or how many different fantasies they would manage to fulfill in the coming days, Rex could already feel the bond between the three of them. It was strong. He doubted he would ever stand on equal ground with them. And that was okay for now. Charlotte apparently needed to experiment, and Rex was introducing himself to the possibility of sharing a woman with other men. So far, he was surprisingly calm.

Her smile grew again. It was for him. But in a moment, she would grant two other men that same smile. Rex didn't believe this arrangement would work forever, but he'd rationalized that he did click with both Samson and Nile, so he could slide into their lives for a while, give Charlotte something she craved, and learn something about himself at the same time.

It might hurt when he eventually left, but it would be a sweet pain that would hold amazing memories.

"We can discuss this in more detail if you'd like," Rex pointed out, taking her pulse. "I realize you're a bit blindsided here."

She shook her head. "I'm good, Sir. Just surprised. In a good way. Amazing Christmas present."

He smiled as he threaded his fingers in her hair, giving it a slight tug backward.

Her sweet lips parted and her eyes rolled back under his control.

"Speaking of Christmas... Based on the number of boxes stacked inside the front door, I'd say we have some decorating to do around here. It's Christmas Eve. Why isn't there a tree up yet?" he teased, his lips coming down to connect with hers briefly.

"Now?" she asked, slightly dazed. "Sir?"

He nodded. "Now. If you're good, maybe I'll come up with some way to reward you after we turn this place into a winter wonderland."

Nile clapped his hands together. "Agreed. Let's get to work."

"Couldn't agree more," Samson added.

Ten minutes later, the room was littered with boxes Rex learned had come from their storage unit downstairs. Most of the contents were decorations the three of them had accumulated over the past three Christmases. Rex was impressed with how much stuff they had amassed.

With all four of them working, they had the tree up and decorated in no time. It was actually fun. Sort of an ice breaker for Rex. He learned that Nile liked to touch Charlotte every chance he got. A caress or a soft kiss. Samson had more of a tendency to swat her butt when she walked by. Both reached beneath her robe to stroke her skin with frequency also.

They each told stories about different ornaments as they unwrapped them, laughing and reminiscing as if they'd been together far longer than three years. It was sweet and endearing. They included Rex in their conversations, but it would take time for him not to feel like an outsider.

Rex slowly joined their dynamic. When Nile finished stringing the lights around the tall artificial tree, and Samson headed for a switch on the wall to make sure it worked, Rex wrapped an arm around Charlotte from behind and hauled her against his chest.

She relaxed into him, tipping her head to one side when he kissed her neck. "I'm so glad you're here, Sir," she murmured.

"Me too." He stroked the underside of her breast with his thumb. He couldn't wait to dominate her.

"You're not nervous here, Sir," she pointed out, twisting her head around to face him. "I mean that in a good way. Inside this house, I'm everyone's submissive."

He nodded. "I get that vibe. And you're right, it puts me in a dominant mode. Don't you forget it," he teased, giving her breast a squeeze before releasing her. "Let's finish turning this place into Christmas so I can show you how dominant I can be."

A half an hour later, they turned the lights out and stood in the center of the room letting the magic of twinkling lights, sparkling ornaments, and dancing candles lure them into a sense of peace.

Charlotte stepped into Rex's arms, tipping her head back to look up at him. "Thank you for being here. Best Christmas present ever."

Samson cleared his throat. "No one has dominated her today. How about you put her out of her misery?"

"I could do that." Rex tugged her hair. "Is that what you want, Charlotte?"

"Yes, Sir." Her voice was breathy. The slight command he had over her already affected her.

"You like a little pain, don't you?"

"Yes, Sir." Her eyes rolled back.

"Safeword?"

"Red, Sir." She licked her lips. It was so gorgeous the way she obviously craved dominance in its many forms.

Rex hadn't expected to walk into the penthouse and so quickly take charge of her, but he was beyond willing. His dick was hard, reminding him how she affected him.

Still holding her hair in his fist, he tugged the sash of her robe free and then eased his hand up her belly until he cupped her breast. He watched her face closely as he pinched her nipple next, slowly at first and then applying more pressure until she gasped and lifted onto her toes.

Her hands were fisted at her sides.

Yep. She enjoyed a bit of pain. He'd known that, of course, from flogging and paddling her, but the way she slid so easily into subspace was impressive.

Rex finally released her nipple and smoothed his hand up to

her shoulder, pushing the silk off so that it fell to the floor. He leaned toward her and spoke close to her ear. "I bet you'd enjoy having these pink buds clamped while I swat your bottom."

She whimpered, a delicious shudder shaking her frame.

Rex glanced at Samson and then Nile, shocked by how calm he felt with the two of them watching. It shouldn't be weird. Not really. They'd invited him into their home to please their submissive. They would clearly give her the moon.

Nile nodded at Rex before shuffling toward the entrance. A moment later, he returned and set a bag down next to Rex —the toy bag Rex had brought with him. "If you need anything, I'm sure we have it in the house," he pointed out as he returned to his spot.

Not surprising.

Rex eased his grip on her hair and tipped her head forward so that she was facing the floor. He released her to grab his bag and set it on the coffee table. He knew exactly what he wanted, and a moment later he had a pair of clothespin style clamps jingling in his hand.

Charlotte flinched when he rounded to her front and cupped her breasts back and forth with one hand, weighing them, teasing them, making her nipples stiffer without contact. He made her wait, knowing the anticipation was half the fun. Finally, he pinched one and drew it out from her breast, quickly clamping it with the rubber tips.

She drew in a sharp breath and held it while he treated the other nipple to the same delicious torture.

Rounding behind her, he slid a palm up and down her back. She was facing the seat of the sectional where she'd been sitting when he came in. "Lean over. Elbows on the cushion. Tits hanging free. Legs straight. Feet wide."

She gracefully obeyed, her hair falling over her shoulders

to curtain her face. He didn't mind. Not this time. It would give her some shred of privacy.

After rummaging through his bag again, he pulled out a short crop with a flat leather square on the end. He held it up for Samson and Nile to see, a brow lifted in question.

They both nodded their consent. It wasn't so much that Rex needed their permission. He was more concerned about whether or not she'd been tapped with a crop before. Based on their reaction, he would assume yes.

Charlotte had no idea what he was holding, so she tensed as he stood to one side of her and set a palm on her lower back. Her ass was so fucking sexy. Smooth white skin. Sensitive. It would have raised pink squares on it in a few minutes.

The first tap he gave her was just hard enough to make her flinch and suck in a breath. She somehow managed to keep her heels on the floor, which also spoke volumes about how experienced she was with submission.

He swatted her again on the other butt cheek, harder this time.

Charlotte managed to remain steady, though he was pretty sure she was holding her breath.

Deciding she could handle more, Rex rained several strikes along her bottom and the backs of her thighs. He watched her closely for signs of losing her composure. Everyone had a breaking point when they would jerk out of the path of a striking object, no matter how trained they were.

When her bottom was officially covered with raised red squares, he paused and flattened his palm on her heated skin, soothing it while she took deep breaths.

Nile came closer. He pulled the coffee table over so that it was a few feet behind her and sat on the edge. He patted the surface next to him and glanced at Samson, who then joined him in that prime viewing location.

"That is so incredibly sexy, baby," Nile said. "Do you mind if I take a few pictures so you can see the progression later?"

"No, Sir. I don't mind."

Nile held up his phone, and Rex leaned out of his line of sight so he could take the photos. Nile was right. Her bottom was beyond fucking hot.

"Damn," Samson murmured. "You might have to teach me how you do that. I'm far more comfortable with my hand than trying to strike precisely while gripping something."

Rex gave him a nod and then turned his attention back to Charlotte. "Can you take more?"

"Yes, Sir." Her voice was strong enough to be believable.

He swatted higher now, covering the untouched parts of her white skin, pinkening her everywhere until it looked like a giant handful of pink tiles had been dropped on the surface. He was careful not to break her skin, but he wanted to push her at the same time, make her squirm.

She was panting now, but still in control.

With a glance at Samson and Nile, Rex increased the pressure, his next swat landing on top of several others hard enough to finally make her lift onto her toes. *There. God, that's hot.*

Usually, when Rex worked with a sub, he followed all the same exact steps as he had this time. His goal with a crop was to slowly bring her to her toes, literally. He loved the control he had and how precisely he could strike a submissive's skin until they flinched. He loved the way they gasped when they finally tipped right to the edge of what they could handle.

Working with Charlotte was different because it wasn't just affecting her; it was also affecting him. His cock was hard and pressing against his jeans. This wasn't the sort of scene he was used to in a club that would end in her walking away, leaving him pleased with his ability. This was the sort of scene where he was going to orgasm in the end.

"Gorgeous," Samson whispered.

As she flattened her feet on the floor, Rex lowered the crop to her thighs again, tapping between them now, knowing she would be aroused.

Sure enough she whimpered as he tapped higher, back and forth, inches from her pussy.

"Drop your forehead to the cushion, baby. Feet wider," Niles demanded.

Charlotte followed his directions without hesitation, and damn but she was even sexier. Her ass was higher now, and all Rex had to do was squat down to see her glistening lower lips. He considered tapping her clit with the crop, but this time he wanted her to come on his fingers. He wanted to feel her orgasm. So, he set the crop down, kept a hand on her lower back, and reached between her legs to stroke his fingers through her folds. "So wet," he whispered.

Charlotte moaned but didn't move.

Neither Samson nor Nile said a word. They'd given Rex all the permission he needed during their numerous phone calls. He didn't look to them now. Instead he concentrated on how hot and needy she was. When he eased a finger into her, he was surprised to find her tight and able to grip him.

His cock ached now. It could wait.

When he removed his finger, he used it to circle her clit, gently, slowly, knowing she would probably come with very little contact.

She moaned louder the moment he stroked the swollen bundle of nerves, her head rolling back and forth against the cushion. Her tits swayed with every movement, the little clamps rocking back and forth.

Rex needed to watch her come as much as he needed to come himself. So, he thrust two fingers into her as deep as possible, and flattened his thumb on her clit.

She cried out and arched her neck, lifting her face as her orgasm consumed her.

And blessed angels, he could feel each pulse of her channel around his fingers. Tight. Throbbing. Soaked.

As she was coming down, Rex reached under her and unclamped one nipple.

Her entire body stiffened as she screamed, her pussy gripping his fingers yet again, one orgasm turning into two and then three.

Through the waves of her pleasure, he unclamped the other nipple seconds later, pinching the swollen bud to ease the pain. His other hand still cupped her pussy, fingers inside, thumb stroking her clit until she winced. Even then, he simply eased his thumb to one side, trapping her warmth with his palm.

He leaned closer and kissed the side of her neck. "That was so beautiful. You can come to your knees now." He removed his fingers and helped her lower her shaking body to her knees. Her elbows still rested on the cushion, and he didn't say a word when she lowered even farther so that she sat on her heels.

Nile leaned over Rex's bag and then grabbed a hand towel. He tossed it toward him. Rex first brought his fingers to his mouth, tasting and inhaling her essence before drying his hand.

After stroking Charlotte's back for a few minutes, Rex was surprised to find her rising to her knees and facing him. She had a very sated happy look on her face.

He brushed her hair back and tucked it behind her ears.

Samson grabbed a bottle of water from the end table and handed it to Rex.

Rex held the back of her head and encouraged her to drink. "Would you like a blanket? Are you cold?"

When she finished sipping and faced him, she rocked his

world. "Actually, Sir, if it pleases you, I'd like to remove your clothes and kneel before you."

He concealed a groan, reminded once again what an amazing submissive she was. He held out both hands at his sides and nodded. "Go for it." Although he'd seen her sweet body naked or nearly so several times, she had not seen his.

Rex took a deep breath and closed his eyes for a moment, focusing on the woman in front of him and how her sweet fingers pulled his shirt over his head and then flattened her palms on his chest. It was hard to believe this woman was the same cheerleader he'd once tutored in physics. The girl he'd erroneously assumed was stuck-up before he got to know her. She'd made him feel incredibly validated and empowered that first day he sat down to tutor her, and she was doing the same now. She leaned in close to flick her tongue over his nipple and then scrape it with her teeth.

Rex groaned as his dick throbbed. He slid his hands up her arms and threaded his fingers in her hair as he tipped his face down to inhale her vanilla scent.

A voice from just a few feet away reminded him that he was not alone with Charlotte. "Enough teasing, sweetheart. Take his pants off," Samson instructed.

Rex rose to his feet, kicked off his shoes, and let Charlotte work on his button and zipper. As she tugged his jeans down, freeing his engorged cock, Nile stepped behind her and gathered her hair away from her face. He secured it with a band at the nape of her neck and then leaned over and kissed the top of her head. "Show him how good you are with your mouth, baby."

Rex shuddered as he stepped out of his jeans. He'd never dreamed of being in a position like this. He'd been sucked off in clubs before. He'd even had sex with an audience. But never had he fucked a woman who currently belonged to two other people while they watched. He wasn't judging their kink though. Never.

As Charlotte began to explore his cock and balls with her gentle fingers, Rex shifted his gaze from her to her Doms. They had both removed their shirts and were undoing their pants. Impressive erections freed, they each stroked themselves.

Rex returned his attention to the sub on her knees, his hand going to her neck. "Suck me, Charlotte."

She drew him into her mouth with enough initial pressure to make him come if he didn't stop her.

He squeezed her neck. "Gentle. I want to enjoy this for a few minutes before you swallow me." When he realized his legs were not going to hold him up under her exploration, he shifted their bodies and sat on the couch.

Charlotte continued to lap at his skin, dragging her tongue up his shaft and then licking his balls.

Rex was boneless as he watched Samson and Nile approach, naked now, clearly intending to participate.

Samson set a hand on her shoulder. "Rise to your feet, sweetheart. Spread them wide. Bend at your waist. If you can keep your attention focused on Rex, we'll make you feel so good."

Nile stood to the other side of her, planting a foot between her legs. He reached between her thighs, and whatever he did made her moan around Rex's shaft.

Rex gritted his teeth. He was not going to last. He'd also never shared a woman with anyone before. Not like this. Today, he was checking off all kinds of new kinks.

He found he didn't mind the two naked men behind Charlotte. They were both touching her in ways he currently wasn't able. Samson was fondling her breasts, and Nile was stroking her pussy. Both acts made her hotter and increased her obvious pleasure at sucking Rex off.

Her fingers dug into his thighs as she licked and suckled him as if her were her last meal. She squirmed her sweet body as her other Doms tormented her with their fingers.

The sound of a condom wrapper made her moan, the vibrations dragging Rex closer to the edge.

When Nile lined his cock up with her entrance from behind, Charlotte lowered her mouth over Rex's dick. So deep he hit the back of her throat.

Rex cupped her face, forcing himself to keep from coming while Samson leaned close enough to draw her nipple into his mouth and Nile eased in and out of her pussy, his hands on her hips.

Charlotte whimpered repeatedly, the urgency in her voice filling the room and sliding up his spine. Rex's balls drew up tight and he pursed his lips, unable to hold back another moment. "Gonna come, Charlotte," he warned her.

She drew him in deeper, hollowing her cheeks.

He finally let go, coming so hard his vision swam, while she worked him, sucking, licking, swallowing. He blinked at her, his fingers sliding to her shoulders as she released him and rested her cheek on his thigh. He stroked her face, watching her expression as Nile thrust into her harder and faster.

When her mouth opened on a long moan, Rex held her steady, enjoying the pure bliss on her face as she came around Nile's erection at the same time Nile obviously emptied himself into the condom.

Before she fully came down from her high, Nile removed himself and Samson took his place behind her. He rolled on a condom and entered her so fast she didn't have time to miss the stretch from Nile's shaft.

Rex held her against his lap, his glance going to Samson as the man sucked a thumb into his mouth and then lowered it to her tight rear hole.

Charlotte squirmed her bottom against Samson's erection as he tapped her hole and then slid his thumb into her.

She cried out and then licked her lips, her hands coming to Rex's thighs, gripping. Her body stiffened. Her eyes rolled back. And Rex just watched. Mesmerized by how everything around him flowed like a perfect machine.

As he witnessed Samson's orgasm and yet another pulled from Charlotte, he knew he was seeing something incredibly special. These three had a bond like nothing he'd ever seen. He was an invited guest. Welcomed into their home to give their submissive an erotic scene. It was hot as fuck. Rex was comfortable and at ease. He would never forget this. But did he belong in this family unit for more than a visit?

CHAPTER 17

Charlotte slowly came awake Christmas morning, realizing she was in the guest room, and Rex's warm body was wrapped around hers. At one point, Nile and Samson had been there too, stroking her skin, whispering soft words, kissing her everywhere. This morning, however, the two of them were not present.

Rex's fingers were dancing up and down her arm, his lips nibbling at her neck. "Merry Christmas," he whispered.

She smiled as she snuggled her back against his front. "Merry Christmas to you too." What a gift. Her heart swelled at the thought of how much time and commitment it had taken for Samson and Nile to arrange this. For her. Because they loved her this much. And she loved them both just as fiercely.

"I smell coffee," Rex murmured. "Let's drag ourselves to the kitchen."

She inhaled deeply, enjoying this moment. She liked the feel of Rex's smooth fingers on her, but she was also eager to wrap her arms around her Doms and thank them for this amazing gift. "Mmm. Sounds good."

Rex kissed her shoulder soundly and then slid out from under the covers.

She rolled onto her back and watched him drag on black sweatpants in the dim light of the room.

When he held out a robe, she finally reached out and let him pull her to standing. He settled the robe on her shoulders and tied the sash at her waist before taking her by the hand and dragging her from the room.

Nile was at the stove, and he lifted his gaze and smiled. "Merry Christmas."

All three of them responded in kind as Charlotte made her way first to Samson who sat perched on a bar stool. She ran her hands up his bare chest and kissed his lips. "I love you."

"I love you too, sweetheart."

"Hey, do I get some of that?" Nile asked. He set a spatula down and grabbed her from behind, making her giggle as he kissed her neck. "I love you too, baby," he murmured.

"I love you," she responded. When she turned around, she found Rex leaning on his elbows on the edge of the island. He was smiling. Happy.

Thank God there was nothing awkward about this arrangement. No one looked the least bit put out. There was definitely an elephant in the room in the form of many questions about what the future would hold, but Charlotte knew only time would give them answers. For now, all was right with the world. It was Christmas morning. She had everything she could ever want in life. It was snowing outside. And no one had to work today.

Charlotte's heart was full as she ate Nile's amazing brunch surrounded by three men. They all moved to the sectional to open gifts and then snuggle against each other to enjoy goofy Christmas movies. When they got hungry, each of them pitched in to get Christmas dinner on the table. No one bothered to get dressed fancy. They just remained casual and laid back.

Charlotte's butt was still sore from the crop the night before, so when they suggested moving to Samson's bedroom, each Dom took a turn examining her to decide what she could tolerate.

In the end, they decided to arrange her on her back and secure her wrists and ankles to the corners of the bed. Nile directed this sensuous scene, which ended up with her writhing beneath the assault of three mouths and six hands. Often in the last few years she'd found herself in this same position with only two men. The addition of a third was mind blowing. And the sensations heightened when Nile added a blindfold, making it impossible for her to predict when someone might thrust into her or lick her most erogenous zones.

By the time she was on her third orgasm, she'd lost track of who had been inside her and which of them had also come. She was once again so sated and relaxed when they finished that she curled onto her side and slept hard, warm bodies at her back and front.

The perfect Christmas day.

CHAPTER 18

On the third morning in the penthouse, Rex lay alone in the guest room, staring up at the ceiling. There were no words to describe what he'd experienced since joining this polyamorous unit. He'd observed and participated in more new scenes than cumulatively in all his years in the lifestyle.

Charlotte was a breath of fresh air. She brought light to every room she entered. When she wasn't home—because she'd gone to work for at least a few hours every day—the entire house felt like it sagged a bit. At least from Rex's perspective.

He got along fantastically with Samson and Nile, and had spent time alone with both of them. They'd kept their conversations light, no one questioning him or pressuring him. No one suggesting he should stay or leave. They weren't going to make choices for him. He needed to figure out his role in this unit on his own.

A knock sounded at the door, and Rex shifted his gaze that direction. "Come in."

Charlotte stepped inside. She held out a mug of coffee as he slid his body up to sitting, resting against the headboard.

"Thought you might like coffee, Sir." She climbed up next to him but then sat with her legs crossed, not touching him, fingering the sheets, her gaze downcast.

Rex took a sip of the fortifying liquid and broke the silence. "Talk to me. As equals." He didn't want her submitting to him while they spoke.

She lifted her gaze and licked her lips. "I was wondering what you're thinking. I love having you here. We all do. And maybe it's too soon to make any suggestions, but I'm hoping you might consider staying."

He swallowed the emotion that welled up inside him and reached out to stroke her cheek. "I can't answer that right now. It's like a honeymoon period. We've had so much fun. I'm still adjusting to the concept. You've all made me feel welcome here, but the three of you are a unit, Charlotte." He kept his voice light and smiled to soften his words.

She nodded, biting into her bottom lip.

"While I'm in awe of you and totally in lust..." He offered a smile. "I can tell that the three of you are in love with each other. It's in your eyes. It's in your actions. You're a family unit. I'm an outsider."

She shook her head. "I don't want you to feel that way. None of us do."

He smiled again. "I know. It's not something you can control." He shifted to one side and set his mug on the bedside table before hauling her onto his lap and brushing her hair from her face. "Have you considered the possibility that it's not me specifically you crave but an open sexual relationship in general? One where you occasionally get a boost from an outside experience. Sometimes that might be a day or a night. Other times, like this time, it might last longer." He tried to sound non-judgmental. Just an observation.

She stiffened, lifting her gaze. Her silk robe was forest

green this morning and it slid off one shoulder to expose her creamy skin. "What do you mean?"

"I mean maybe you enjoy a life with multiple men and need something fresh and new every now and then." He schooled his voice, watching her carefully. "I know you think it's *me* you crave, Charlotte, but consider the idea that it's not me specifically. Maybe it's something fresh and new and different. I represent that, and we have a rapport between us, but it's not forever." He'd accepted this fact, just like he'd accepted that he might come and go from these people's lives for a while, but eventually it would end.

She stared at him, but he could see her thinking, pondering his words.

He slid his gaze to her shoulder and then leaned in and kissed her skin, his lips lingering on her, dragging up to her neck and then behind her ear.

When she giggled, ticklish in that spot, he flicked his tongue there, making her scrunch up her shoulders. He leaned back and met her gaze again, cupping her face with one hand while the other was draped around her waist. "You're so sexy. Intoxicating. I love being here with you. I don't even mind sharing you with two other Doms. There is no jealousy in this house. It's refreshing. And I'm learning more about myself with every passing day. How about this..."

She sat straighter, her expression serious.

"You know I travel a lot for work. When I'm not traveling, I usually work from home. How about if I plan to spend part of my time here in Seattle."

She grinned broadly, her eyes widening.

"Don't get carried away. It won't be every week. Some weeks I need to on the road. Next week, for example, I have to be in Boston. I'll need to go to Denver for a few days after that. I skipped out on my family for Christmas. They're going to begin to think I'm leading a secret life."

She giggled. "Aren't you?"

"Well, yes." He shrugged, lifting one corner of his mouth. "But I'm not prepared to explain any of this to them. They just think I had plans with friends, which I did. Naked plans. With floggers and whips," he teased.

"I love your kind of plans."

"Well, my family doesn't even know I belong to a club, let alone that I spent the last three days sharing a sexy submissive with two other men. My mother would faint."

"So, you'll stop by Denver, reassure them you're alive, convince them work has you traveling more than usual, and then join us when you can here in Seattle. Yeah?"

"That's my thinking. I need to run it by Samson and Nile first of course." He tapped her nose. "You're not the only person living here, nor are you in charge by any stretch of the imagination."

Another giggle that made him warm all over.

He held her gaze for a while, realizing that as much as he enjoyed being with her, she didn't belong to him. She belonged to two other men. He'd always known that. It wasn't a revelation. He also knew that one day this arrangement would no longer include him. He would come and go for as long as it worked for everyone involved, but in the end, he would still be the interloper.

It no longer scared the hell out of him that he couldn't have Charlotte as his own. He had a piece of her for now. It was all he needed. He didn't have the sort of job that permitted him to give all of himself to another person anyway. He was out of town too much.

He was enjoying every day that he spent with these three people who were so dedicated to each other. Even if they invited him to stay permanently in a few months, he already knew the answer would be no.

Rex wasn't at all sure what the world had in store for him.

He was learning more about himself as he went along. But Samson, Nile, and Charlotte were a unit. Granted, they were a unit that needed to include other Doms from time to time to fulfill Charlotte's craving for new experiences. But the core unit was solid and intact.

They were so lucky. He would never take his time here for granted.

CHAPTER 19

Six months later…

Charlotte was sitting on the balcony, head tipped back, enjoying a rare sunny warm day in Seattle. She was naked, her robe discarded at her side as she lounged in the sun.

A shadow came over her, and she opened her eyes to find Nile standing in the doorway. "Please tell me you're slathered from head to toe in sunscreen."

"Yes, Sir." She smiled. "I just wanted to feel the warmth."

"Good." He sat on the edge of her lounge chair and dragged his fingers up her body from her thigh to her breast. When he flicked the tips, she moaned. "You are the most sensitive woman alive."

She sighed.

"Why aren't you at work?" he asked.

"Came home early because the sun was out, and all I could think about was lying here naked and waiting for you to get home." She smiled at him, arching her chest into his fingers as they continued to torment her nipple.

"Let me guess, you're hoping I'll make some summer dish for you like pasta salad or hamburgers."

"Both would be great," she suggested.

"Huh. Well, it just so happens that Samson is on his way here too, so you're in luck. I'm going to cook for you, princess." He leaned in and kissed her, and then he rose and left her lying on the balcony.

She stared at the doorway for a moment, watching his fine ass as he left her before closing her eyes once again. She must have drifted off because the next time she awoke, it was to the startled feeling of something very cold dripping on her nipple. She bolted awake, crying out while she swiped at the cool liquid.

Samson was grinning above her. He had a beer in his hand. The condensation had dripped onto her chest, assuredly not by accident.

Nile was on her other side, the smell of the grill filling the air as he turned it on.

"Nice nap?" Samson asked as he took a seat next to her hip, scooting her to one side.

"Yes, Sir."

"Please tell me you're wearing sunscreen," he said, parroting Nile from earlier.

She rolled her eyes. "Guys, give me some credit."

Samson lifted a brow. "Did you just roll your eyes at me and then sass me?"

"Oops. Sorry, Sir." She squirmed, her pussy growing wet at the thought of Samson's palm landing on her bottom. He hadn't spanked her in a few weeks. Sometimes, she thought he set her up for discipline. And frankly, she didn't mind a bit.

"Nile, can you help me out here. I think our girl needs to flip over and get some of the sun's warmth on her backside."

Charlotte bit her lip, trying not to react as Samson pulled her to sitting and then Nile lowered to sit where her back had just been. A moment later, she found herself draped over Nile's lap on her belly, her breasts pressing against his thigh, her hands trapped at the small of her back by Nile's larger ones.

Samson smoothed a palm over her bottom and then reached between her legs. "Already wet for me."

She moaned around the contact, craving whatever he would give her. Even sweet denial was enjoyable to her when she had both men handling her.

The first swat on her bottom still took her breath away. The second was harder and made her stiffen. "God, I love watching your skin pinken, sweetheart."

Nile held her steady while Samson spanked her bottom more times than she could count. Every once in a while, he fingered her, but he didn't let her come.

When he was finished, she was a ball of nerves, so close to orgasm she was shaking. Nile still held her wrists at the small of her back, while Samson spread her legs farther and molded his hands to her heated bottom. His thumbs came close to her tight hole over and over until he finally dragged them through her wetness and then teased her puckered skin. "It's been a while since we were both inside you at once," he pointed out.

She moaned, wiggling against Nile's thighs.

Nile stroked her arm. "Would you like that, baby?"

"Yes, Sir." She enjoyed nothing more than to have them both at once.

Nile lifted her onto her knees and rose to lower his pants down to his thighs. He sat on the lounge chair and reached for her. "Straddle me."

She climbed over him, her bottom stinging from the recent spanking, making her skin heat. Her heart raced at the thought of having her men inside her.

Samson tossed Nile a condom, and she watched as he

rolled it on. He grabbed her hips and lifted her over his shaft. "Just one rule."

She swallowed.

"You don't get to come until both of us do," Nile continued.

Charlotte nodded. It would be difficult. "Yes, Sir."

Nile lowered her onto his cock, filling her so full that she moaned, her eyes already rolling back into her head. He reclined the chair so that it was almost flat behind him and pulled her down to his chest.

Samson played with her pussy, gathering her arousal from around Nile's shaft and dragging it to her tight hole. The condom itself would be lubricated too, so she wasn't worried. They'd played before without lube. When he nudged her entrance, she blew out a breath and relaxed her tight muscles.

Nile soothed her back. "Good girl. Let him in, baby."

Samson took his time, making slow progress. When he was fully seated, both men deep inside her, she closed her eyes and inhaled. There was no better feeling in the world. God, she loved these men.

They gave her a moment to adjust, and then Samson took control, setting a pace, thrusting in and out of her while lifting her on and off Nile's cock. She helped when she got the rhythm, her hands planted on Nile's chest, all of her concentration focused on holding back her need to orgasm.

She ended up holding her breath several times, willing them to both come as soon as possible.

They had other plans though and took their sweet time. When first Samson and then Nile finally let it go, she finally breathed. Her body shook as Samson pulled out of her and took a second to dispose of the condom. When he was back, he wrapped his arms around her, left her impaled by Nile, and held her upright. His lips landed on her ear. "Now, it's your turn sweetheart."

His forearms rested under her breasts, preventing her from watching her connection with Nile, but seconds later, Nile's fingers were on her clit, thrumming it rapidly.

With his cock still deep inside her, she easily rose to the edge of the cliff. And then she was tumbling over the other side, her orgasm shaking her entire body as Nile continued to fondle her, and Samson continued to hold her in place.

Perfection.

Pure bliss.

There was no comparison.

~

An hour later, sated and happy, Charlotte was seated at the round glass table on the deck with a burger and pasta salad in front of her. She was the luckiest sub on the planet.

They ate in peace, teasing each other and discussing their day.

It wasn't until they were finished that Samson leaned back and met her gaze. "I spoke to Rex this morning."

She cocked her head. "Where is he, Sir? How is he doing?"

Samson waved a hand between them. "Frank chat here. Don't submit."

She nodded.

"He's in Miami, actually, and he was kinda vague about what he was doing."

"Has he gone to Club Zodiac there?" Nile asked.

"Yep."

"I bet he's met someone," Charlotte pointed out.

Samson leaned forward. "How does that make you feel?"

She sighed. "I'm okay with it. It was bound to happen eventually."

Nile nodded. "I always thought so too. He's been visiting

less often than he did six months ago. He hasn't been here in six weeks. I tend to agree with Charlotte."

"Or maybe more than one someone," Samson pointed out. He reached across the table and took Charlotte's hand, squeezing it. "You're sure you're good?"

She smiled, meeting his gaze again. "I'm beyond good. I have the best two Doms in the world." She grabbed both of their hands. "I love you both more than words can express. I've known almost from the beginning that Rex would not choose to stay forever."

Nile reached out with his other hand and drew a finger down her cheek. "You enjoy having a fourth now and then though. It was the perfect arrangement because it shook things up just often enough to keep you guessing."

"Yeah, but I don't have to have it. It's not like I'm unhappy if I don't have another Dom commanding me while I have the best two in Seattle at my beck and call," she teased.

Both men slid their chairs closer. There was an awkward silence.

Finally, Samson cleared his throat. "We've been talking."

She lifted both eyebrows, concern consuming her.

Nile continued. "We haven't been to Surrender in a while. We think it's time to venture out again. See what happens. Maybe pick up a fourth for some role play."

Her pulse picked up as she looked at Nile. "Is that what you want?"

He nodded. "It's what we both want. We love you to pieces, and we know you love us too. The need for occasional open playing is a part of you, and we'll fill it every time we think it's necessary."

Samson spoke again. "The rules don't change. We decide when and where and approve of anyone you've got your eyes on. You won't have sex without our permission. You don't get to orgasm without us watching. Panties on. Yada yada. Same as before we met Rex."

She couldn't stop smiling. They understood her so well.

Nile cleared his throat. "I know we sucked at expressing our feelings for far too long, but we'll never do that again. We're a committed ménage. In my heart we are legally bound to each other. It is unlikely we will ever meet a fourth person and invite them to stay forever. It's not really what you need anyway. You need the occasional thrill of excitement from being dominated by someone different. We get it. We'll make it happen."

A tear slid down both her cheeks. Samson and Nile reached at the same time to wipe them away. She glanced from one man to the other, clearing her throat. There was one more thing she wanted to address.

"What else is on your mind?" Samson asked.

"You two."

He lifted a brow, glancing at Nile. "What about us?"

"I know you love each other as much as you love me."

"Of course we do," Nile responded, brows furrowing.

"When are you going to explore something more physical?"

Samson turned to look at Nile again. "We've been talking about that. We know we're emotionally committed. That part's easy, but you're right, we need to see what we might be interested in on a physical level."

"Good. I'd like to be involved in that exploration, if you don't mind." Her heart felt lighter already. The thought of her two Doms crossing over that line was something that made her heart rate pick up. They'd never avoided touching each other affectionately, but she wanted them to consider something more intimate.

Nile gave her hand another squeeze. "I think that can be arranged. Don't you, Samson?"

"Definitely." Samson leaned forward, his face inches from hers.

"I love you both so much," she whispered as they closed the distance and kissed her at the same time.

When all their lips came together, it was like everything was right with the world. Her heart was at peace. Her soul was full.

AUTHOR'S NOTE

I hope you've enjoyed *Sharing Charlotte* from my *Club Zodiac* series. There are nine books total in the series.

Club Zodiac:
Training Sasha
Obeying Rowen
Collaring Brooke
Mastering Rayne
Trusting Aaron
Claiming London
Sharing Charlotte
Taming Rex
Tempting Elizabeth

Please enjoy the following excerpt from *Raising Lucy*, the first book in my *Surrender* series.

RAISING LUCY

SURRENDER, BOOK ONE

"It's done."

I spin my desk chair around to find Julius, the manager of my club and the only man I would trust with the task I've assigned him. He drops a thick file on my desk. "You're sure?" I lift a brow, my heart pounding. If I pull this off...

Julius narrows his gaze. "Roman, you insult me."

I blow out a breath and open the file. Her picture is on top. I run my hands over the page, caressing it. Julius Polk is one of my oldest friends. He's also one of only two people who do not call me Master Roman or Sir. The other is our mutual friend Claudia Renault. Everyone else in my life refers to me using a respectful title.

"You think she'll be here tonight?" I ask, not lifting my gaze from her photo.

"I can't guarantee that, but if she doesn't show, we'll move to plan B or even plan C. This will work."

I nod.

Julius leaves me alone once more in my enormous office on the second story of my Seattle fetish club, Surrender.

I close my eyes, willing my heart to slow down. This

reaction is so unlike me. I don't want any of my employees to see me nervous. I have a reputation in Seattle as one of the most severe Doms. I've earned that reputation intentionally. It's not just a reputation. It's my life. I'm demanding. I'm strict. I get what I want.

And I want Lucy Neill.

She is mine.

She is my girl.

My life.

My world.

She just doesn't know it yet.

ALSO BY BECCA JAMESON

Seattle Doms:

Salacious Exposure by Becca Jameson

Salacious Desires By Kate Oliver

Salacious Attraction by Becca Jameson

Salacious Indulgence by Kate Oliver

Salacious Devotion by Becca Jameson

Salacious Surrender by Kate Oliver

Danger Bluff:

Rocco

Hawking

Kestrel

Magnus

Phoenix

Caesar

Roses and Thorns:

Marigold

Oleander

Jasmine

Tulip

Daffodil

Lily

Roses and Thorns Box Set One

Roses and Thorns Box Set Two

Shadowridge Guardians:

Steele by Pepper North

Kade by Kate Oliver

Atlas by Becca Jameson

Doc by Kate Oliver

Gabriel by Becca Jameson

Talon by Pepper North

Bear by Becca Jameson

Faust by Pepper North

Storm by Kate Oliver

Blade by Pepper North

King by Kate Oliver

Rock by Becca Jameson

Blossom Ridge:

Starting Over

Finding Peace

Building Trust

Feeling Brave

Embracing Joy

Accepting Love

Blossom Ridge Box Set One

Blossom Ridge Box Set Two

The Wanderers:

Sanctuary

Refuge

Harbor

Shelter

Nonstop

Standby

Takeoff

Jetway

Open Skies Box Set One

Open Skies Box Set Two

Shadow SEALs:

Shadow in the Desert

Shadow in the Darkness

Holt Agency:

Rescued by Becca Jameson

Unchained by KaLyn Cooper

Protected by Becca Jameson

Liberated by KaLyn Cooper

Defended by Becca Jameson

Unrestrained by KaLyn Cooper

Delta Team Three (Special Forces: Operation Alpha):

Destiny's Delta

Canyon Springs:

Caleb's Mate

Hunter's Mate

Corked and Tapped:

Volume One: Friday Night

Volume Two: Company Party

Volume Three: The Holidays

The Complete Set

Tempting Elizabeth

Club Zodiac Box Set One

Club Zodiac Box Set Two

Club Zodiac Box Set Three

The Art of Kink:

Pose

Paint

Sculpt

Arcadian Bears:

Grizzly Mountain

Grizzly Beginning

Grizzly Secret

Grizzly Promise

Grizzly Survival

Grizzly Perfection

Arcadian Bears Box Set One

Arcadian Bears Box Set Two

Sleeper SEALs:

Saving Zola

Spring Training:

Catching Zia

Catching Lily

Catching Ava

Spring Training Box Set

The Underground series:

Force

Clinch

Guard

Submit

Thrust

Torque

The Underground Box Set One

The Underground Box Set Two

Wolf Masters series:

Kara's Wolves

Lindsey's Wolves

Jessica's Wolves

Alyssa's Wolves

Tessa's Wolf

Rebecca's Wolves

Melinda's Wolves

Laurie's Wolves

Amanda's Wolves

Sharon's Wolves

Wolf Masters Box Set One

Wolf Masters Box Set Two

Claiming Her series:

The Rules

The Game

The Prize

Claiming Her Box Set

Emergence series:

Bound to be Taken

Bound to be Tamed

Bound to be Tested

Bound to be Tempted

Emergence Box Set

The Fight Club series:

Come

Perv

Need

Hers

Want

Lust

The Fight Club Box Set One

The Fight Club Box Set Two

Wolf Gatherings series:

Tarnished

Dominated

Completed

Redeemed

Abandoned

Betrayed

Wolf Gatherings Box Set One

Wolf Gathering Box Set Two

Durham Wolves series:

Rescue in the Smokies

Fire in the Smokies

Freedom in the Smokies

Durham Wolves Box Set

ABOUT THE AUTHOR

Becca Jameson is a USA Today best-selling author of over 150 books. She is well-known for her Wolf Masters series, her Fight Club series, and her Surrender series. She currently lives in Houston, Texas, with her husband. Two grown kids pop in every once in a while, too! She is loving this journey and has dabbled in a variety of genres, including paranormal, sports romance, military, reverse harem, dark romance, suspense, dystopian, BDSM, and Daddy Dom.

A total night owl, Becca writes late at night, sequestering herself in her office with a glass of red wine and a bar of dark chocolate, her fingers flying across the keyboard as her characters weave their own stories.

During the day--which never starts before ten in the morning!--she can be found walking, running errands, or reading in her favorite hammock chair!

...where Alphas dominate...

Becca's Newsletter Sign-up

Join my Facebook fan group, Becca's Bibliomaniacs, for the most up-to-date information, random excerpts while I work, giveaways, and fun release parties!

Facebook Fan Group:
Becca's Bibliomaniacs

Contact Becca:
www.beccajameson.com
beccajameson4@aol.com

f facebook.com/becca.jameson.18
X x.com/beccajameson
⊙ instagram.com/becca.jameson
BB bookbub.com/authors/becca-jameson
g goodreads.com/beccajameson
a amazon.com/author/beccajameson